A KISS FOR THE AGES

A REGENCY NOVELLA

GRACE BURROWES

GRACE BURROWES PUBLISHING

Copyright © 2025 by Grace Burrowes

All rights reserved.

No part of this book may be reproduced in any form or by any electronic or mechanical means, including information storage and retrieval systems, without written permission from the author, except for the use of brief quotations in a book review.

If you uploaded this book to, or downloaded it from, any free file sharing, internet "archive" library, or other piracy site, you did so in violation of the law and against the author's wishes. No part of this book may be used to train, prompt, or otherwise interact with any large language model generative artificial intelligence program.

Please don't be a pirate.

DEDICATION

Dedicated to those who persevere against the odds

CHAPTER ONE

"I yearn for a daughter I can be proud of," Lysander, Earl of Montmarche said. "I long for my offspring to be respected and admired." He remained calm by sheer force of self-discipline, because shouting at his only female progeny when lecturing her about the need for decorum could prove counterproductive.

His lordship nonetheless longed to bellow and curse, as his own dear papa had bellowed and cursed. Montmarche craved in truth to use language that would inspire Sophronia to feats of mimicry hitherto undreamed of by an English female, much less one only ten years old.

"Lady Sophronia is incorrigible, my lord." Miss Dagmire cast a glance at her unrepentant charge such as teetotaling aunties reserved for habitual drunkards. "She cannot be reformed, despite my unrelenting efforts. My reputation as a governess will be imperiled should I make further attempts. You may consider this notice of my intent to vacate my post."

Lysander allowed that announcement to hang in the air long enough that Miss Dagmire's confident air curdled into pugnacity. He could forbid her to go, but as she'd said, she had failed. They all failed where Sophronia was concerned.

Meaning *he* had failed.

But he would not give up.

"You will remain until I can find a replacement." He'd learned three governesses ago to demand that consideration. The summer Sophronia had been without direct supervision, she'd gone swimming in the mill pond by moonlight, smuggled a pony into the conservatory, and tried to build her own tree house.

"Your lordship will need only long enough to write me a character," Miss Dagmore retorted.

Sophronia stared mulishly at her toes, sitting still as a mouse in a room full of cats. A leaf had caught in one of her braids, and her pinafore bore a green stain at the back.

"If you expect a glowing character when you've given up less than three months after taking a position, then the least you can do is remain until the wedding celebration has concluded. You may be excused."

Miss Dagmire sniffed, curtseyed with less than studied grace, and marched for the door.

When Lysander was alone with his daughter, he let another silence build, though Sophronia was learning how to deal with even those. She remained quiet and motionless, and more than all of her disobedience and wayward behavior, the silence tore at him.

Your mother would despair of you. Unfair, because had Marie lived, Sophronia would have had her mother's loving hand to guide her. Lysander would have had a wife's counsel to guide *him,* and no pony smuggling or moonlit swims would have occurred.

"Have you anything to say?" he asked.

"I'm sorry, Papa, but George can smoke cigars and he refused to let me have a puff of one of his. He is my brother, so if he won't share with me, then nobody will."

George is a man. How many times had Lysander resorted to that excuse? "He is two-and twenty, you are ten. At ten, he did not smoke cigars. I did not smoke cigars at such a tender age, and I still regard them as an execrable habit. In all of England, I doubt there is a ten-year-old female who willingly partakes of cigars."

She turned a hopeful, pansy-blue gaze on him. "Will you teach me how to smoke when I'm eleven?"

The moment ought to have been comical, a small, grass-stained female bargaining her way to hoyden-hood with her titled father.

"You stole from me," Lysander said. "Took a cigar without permission from my humidor. You left the nursery without permission—"

"I had permission, Papa. Miss Dagmire takes tea at 3 o'clock. If I complete my sums early then I am allowed to sit in the garden beneath the nursery windows for twenty minutes while Henderson sits with me. Henderson meets me in the garden, so I nicked your cigar when I was—"

She bowed her head and hunched in on herself.

"At least you admit your crime, though your honesty is the smallest of consolations amid a sea of disappointments, Sophronia." *What am I to do with you?*

Lysander no longer posed that rhetorical question. Sophronia's suggestions in response had included sending her to live in America *with the bears*, banishing her to the home farm *all summer*, or making her dress *as a boy* and work in the stables.

The child was as unlike her father as it was possible for offspring to be.

"I'm sorry, Papa."

Don't be sorry. Be normal. Be a little girl who reads fairytales and practices walking about the schoolroom with a book on her head. Every governess seemed to feel that skill was an imperative accomplishment, along with needlepoint, small talk, and sitting still.

Lysander was saved from trotting out the rest of his usual sermon by the sound of carriage wheels on the drive. Sophronia's head jerked up, but she remained otherwise motionless.

"The wedding guests are due to start arriving at any moment," he said. "Your stunt is as usual exquisitely timed to cause maximum disruption, but don't think to escape punishment, Sophronia. You stole from your own father, and that requires more than a mere apology."

"Yes, Papa."

But how to make the punishment fit the crime? When George had started pilfering brandy and cigars, he'd been fourteen, and Lysander had overlooked the transgressions. Boys experimented, and better that they experiment before they were packed off to learn the usual vices at university.

He came around his desk to loom over Sophronia. She did not have his height, yet anyway, for which God be thanked.

"You will write an essay about the Great London Fire," he said. "You will research the devastation, the lives and houses lost, the impact on London thereafter. You will present the fruits of your scholarship to me at this time tomorrow, not a blot on the entire page. You will have no pudding with your supper for the next week, and you will no longer be allowed to travel from the nursery to the garden on your own."

With a house full of guests, permitting that folly would have been madness.

"But may I still sit in the garden? Please, Papa. It's only twenty minutes."

She loved to be out of doors, much as her mother had. *Maria, I don't know what to do.*

He laid a hand on Sophronia's slender shoulder and gently squeezed. "You may sit in the garden..."

The child drew in her breath and squirmed under his hand.

Dear God, not this too. "Sophronia, you have already fallen short of standards by stealing. Do not think to lie to me now. Has Miss Dagmire resorted to corporal punishment in her frustration with you?"

Sophronia looked up and stared at him as if he'd slipped a complicated French phrase into the conversation.

"Does she beat you?" Lysander asked, kneeling down to his daughter's eye level. "Do not think to lie, child, or I'll have Henderson inspect your unclothed person."

Sophronia pulled the leaf from her braid. "Miss Dagmire does not beat me. She applies a birch rod for the sake of my soul. She gives me twelve stripes, though I deserve thirty at least, and if I think to earn your sympathy by complaining to you she'll give me twelve more."

The carriage wheels on the crushed shells crunched to a halt. The flood of guests had begun, and the mischief Sophronia would be tempted to get into would be limitless.

"Henderson will not simply supervise you in the garden," Lysander said. "She will attend you at all times, because you cannot be trusted to comport yourself as a lady ought. You are excused. Tell Miss Dagmire to await me in the schoolroom after I've greeted my guests."

And tell her to pack her bags.

Sophronia popped off her chair. "I'm to write an essay on the Great Fire, not have any pudding, and keep company with Henderson. Is there anything else, Papa?"

Anymore, Lysander saw his daughter mostly to rebuke her. She seemed eager to leave his company, and he had guests to welcome. Still, the moment called for some further comment, some paternal display.

"If you are well behaved for the duration of the wedding party, then I will consider allowing you to resume your riding lessons."

Sophronia launched herself at him, lashing her arms about his waist, squeezing him as if he'd conjured a magic coach drawn by matching pink unicorns.

"Thank you, Papa! I shall be the best girl ever, and you will be so proud of me!"

She skipped from the room as no lady ought to skip, pausing at the door to beam at him, before closing the door much too enthusiastically. A carriage door banged shut immediately afterward, and hoofbeats clip-clopped in the direction of the stables.

Lysander paused long enough to regard himself in the mirror over the sideboard. He did not look like a man who'd fought two domestic skirmishes, discovered grounds to sack another governess, and delivered stern terms of surrender to the rebellious infantry.

He looked like a man who very much still missed the wife who'd died ten years ago. Maria smiled down from her place over the mantel, eternally serene, ever the woman who'd captured his heart. She'd been stealthy and sweet about it, until Lysander had looked up from his bacon and eggs one morning two years after the wedding, and realized that he'd fallen in love with his countess.

He wanted that for his children. A solid, happy match of esteem, affection, and abiding respect.

He didn't particularly want to remarry himself, but Sophronia's latest prank removed the last doubt. He'd considered the list of guests invited to his niece's wedding carefully, and with matrimony in the air, he would select a suitable step-mama for his wayward daughter.

That he'd have to marry the lady could not be avoided. If Lysander believed in one tenet above all others, it was that a man born to privilege must never shirk an obligation to a dependent. He owed it to his daughter to remarry, before the dear child burned England to cinders, and sent her father's dignity up in flames as well.

～

"Promise me you will not consume brandy in company, Mama." Phoebe's demand, the last of many, was made as Daphne Cargill's coach rattled through the gate posts of the Earl of Montmarche's estate.

The usual lions couchant sat atop the usual pillars leading onto the usual crushed shell drive.

"I make you that most solemn oath." Daphne had sneaked a draught of Lady Bellefonte's excellent brandy on an occasion two years past. How was she to have known that Miss Threadlebaum and Miss Anastasia Arbuckle had been lurking among the racy French poets?

"And you won't start political arguments either, Mama."

"I never start political arguments. Some fool makes a deliberately provocative statement and requires correction." Usually a male fool, those being generally more vocal than the female variety, and in polite society, more abundant as well.

Phoebe rubbed gloved fingers across her forehead. "The Earl of Montmarche is not a fool, Mama. He's wealthy, titled, respected, and the uncle of the bride. You vex our host at my peril."

"*I* am wealthy, titled, and respected." A slight mis-statement. Daphne was monied and a viscount's widow, which meant her idiosyncrasies were tolerated by her in-laws, provided she remained within the bounds of decorum.

The Earl of Montmarche, whatever his other qualities, owned a beautiful corner of England. The coach wound through acres of grazed parkland, fluffy sheep dotting a green expanse. Stands of trees interrupted the rolling carpet of grass, and a sizeable lake mirrored the blue summer sky.

"This terrain has not been forcibly landscaped," Daphne observed, pushing the leather curtain farther aside. "The hand of man did not fashion this ground to suit human aesthetics." In the last century, taming nature had become an expensive passion among the very wealthy, with the result that many estates had taken on the quality of a youth forced to sit for a portrait.

Dull, predictable, and to Daphne's eye sullen and blighted. Montmarche's property was still exuberantly bucolic, bordered by woods that doubtless threatened to encroach on the meadow year by year.

"Mama, *please*. You must school your features to a pleasant expression. Nobody likes an eccentric grouch."

"I'm lost in thought," Daphne replied. "Where to put my easel, which vista to capture first? You needn't fret, my dear. I will behave." For her children's sake, Daphne had been behaving for years.

Phoebe's expression was more worried than pleasant. "Three Seasons, Mama. I'm an heiress who has failed to secure a match despite being out for *three* Seasons. I have all the pretty dresses, I am accounted a competent horsewoman. I practice my pianoforte diligently, and never stumble on the dance floor. If I am not married by next spring, or at least engaged, I must retire to the country."

Such a dire fate, to be surrounded by rural friends, peace, and fresh air. "I did not meet your father until I was three-and-twenty, Phoebe." A reminder that never seemed to comfort the firstborn of that union, but Daphne did not know what else to say. Phoebe's fear of spinsterhood was reinforced at every social gathering, in every gossip column, and by an endless stream of unkind talk.

"You were fabulously wealthy, Mama. You could be choosy."

The coach swayed around a bend in the lane and the enormous yellow granite façade of Marche Hall came into view. The building was like the landscape—asymmetric, unapologetic, and quietly magnificent. Previous earls had clearly added on and added on again, though they'd done so with an eye toward balance and form. The grounds flowed into manicured parterres and low hedges flanking the circular drive, and sunlight bounced off scores of gleaming windows.

"I shall be lost before supper," Phoebe observed.

"You will have time to rest before we meet the other guests," Daphne retorted as the coach slowed to take its place behind two others. "Grand edifices like this usually follow a logical plan, and the only complicated parts are where one wing joins another. I won't let you become lost."

At some point in the past three years, Phoebe herself had nonetheless become bewildered, and Daphne didn't know what to do about that either. Daphne had been a spectacularly wealthy bride, true, but Phoebe's status as an heiress was also beyond dispute.

And yet, Phoebe viewed herself as a wallflower-in-waiting.

"He's on the terrace." Phoebe let the window shade on her side of the coach drop. "The earl himself is greeting guests in person. Mama, I look a fright, and he's Miss Gavineau's uncle. I shall make a terrible first impression."

"A gracious host greets guests, Phoebe. That's no great feat of hospitality." Montmarche was in riding attire, a tall, trim figure going gray about the temples. He bowed over the hand of a woman in a blue coaching dress, the gesture correct without being fawning. "Mrs. Cavanaugh is here."

"Her younger sister is one of Miss Gavineau's friends. I like Mrs. Cavanaugh."

Meaning Mrs. Cavanaugh had never been caught tippling brandy because monthly pangs of the womb threatened to rob her of consciousness half-way through a dinner party.

"She is all that is admirable." Emma Cavanaugh had buried two husbands after providing them each an heir and a spare. At thirty, she was pretty, charming, and once again out of mourning.

Daphne wished her good hunting.

"Montmarche is handsome," Phoebe said, peering through the gap between the shade and the window glass, "in a distinguished sort of way."

Daphne left off gathering up her reticule, bonnet, and gloves long enough to study Montmarche. He was still chatting with Mrs. Cavanaugh, and they'd been joined by a younger man who bore a resemblance to the earl.

A portrait of Montmarche indoors would feature the usual testaments to aristocratic male consequence: A bust of some philosopher, learned tomes, heavy furniture, and heavier symbolism. Out of doors he'd be posed with a handsome fowling piece, a loyal hound or two, and very likely another marble bust. Perhaps a snorting steed might figure into the composition, because some aspect of an outdoor portrait must have a bit of life.

All in all, he'd make a dull subject. He was not precisely handsome. His features leaned toward boldness—a slight hook to the nose, the eyes a trifle deep-set, the mouth severe—but a lack of animation took a fierce countenance and made it merely serious.

Phoebe was retying her bonnet ribbons, because even the size and angle of the bow beneath a young woman's chin was a matter of importance to her, while Daphne looped her reticule over her wrist, grabbed her parasol and rose.

A liveried footman opened the door and lowered the steps, and Daphne prepared to negotiate her descent. Too many hours of sitting had taken a toll on her joints, and the afternoon sunshine was bright after the gloom inside the coach.

Nonetheless, fresh air was always a joy. Daphne gathered her skirts, took the footman's gloved hand, and stepped down. She anticipated putting her boot on *terra firma* just as Phoebe's foot came down on the back of Daphne's skirts.

The result was an awkward careen into the footman's chest, followed by Phoebe's loudly distressed, "Mama! Have a care!"

Montmarche looked up from his conversation, though it was the young man at his side who bounded down the steps.

"Madam, is aught amiss? Why must coach steps be so treacherous? George Marche at your service. Welcome to Montmarche. Are you able to stand? I hope you haven't turned an ankle. Please say you have not." He was ginger-haired and painfully young, also—it appeared—sincerely concerned.

"I simply mis-stepped, Mr. Marche, a lamentably frequent occurrence. I am nonetheless happy to be free of the coach." Daphne stepped aside so that Phoebe could exit the vehicle. Nobody was on hand to make introductions, which was sometimes the way when a house party began. "I am Daphne, Lady Cargill."

"Allow me," Mr. Marche said, offering Phoebe his arm. "You must be Miss Cargill. Welcome to Montmarche."

The Cargill title was one of few that exactly matched the family name, a situation that occasioned confusion more often than not. Mr. Marche had clearly acquainted himself with the guest list, which spoke in his favor.

The earl remained on the terrace, Mrs. Cavanaugh's hand wrapped about his elbow. His lordship was neither smiling nor scowling, while Emma Cavanaugh had clearly enjoyed Daphne's stumbling. Emma wasn't mean, but she was shrewd and pragmatic.

"Mrs. Cavanaugh," Daphne called. "A pleasure to see you." A pleasure to surprise the woman with a bit of forwardness as well. The proper, polite thing to do was wait for the earl to acknowledge his most recent arrivals, but standing around on the drive like a nervous candidate from an employment agency was not in Daphne's nature.

"Lady Cargill." Mrs. Cavanaugh curtsied and resumed her hold of the earl. "My lord, allow me to conduct introductions, if you and Lady Cargill are not acquainted."

Daphne climbed the steps on the arm of the footman while Mr. Marche escorted Phoebe. Mrs. Cavanaugh was staking a claim, positioning herself as hostess, as the woman with authority to introduce Montmarche to his own guests.

Montmarche, for his part, looked oblivious to the fact that he was being claimed. If anything, he looked bored.

The introductions proceeded predictably, with Phoebe offering a painfully correct curtsey. The earl bowed at the appropriate time, he recited an appropriate welcome. His manner was dignified without being warm, and if he minded Mrs. Cavanaugh clinging to him like a limpet fastened to the only rock in the harbor, he gave no sign of it.

Daphne might have dismissed him as yet another dull aristocrat, except that when a shrill, protracted scream rent the air, he bolted into the house with the speed of a man half his age.

Not quite so dull, then, if he was willing to leave Emma Cavanaugh gaping alone on the steps. Not quite so dull, after all.

CHAPTER TWO

Lysander took the main stairs two at a time, certain no housemaid had let loose with that cry. The pitch was too high, the terror too palpable. He gained the top of the steps and came upon Sophronia gaping at the circular window that looked out over the drive.

"Young lady," he said, rather loudly. "Explain yourself."

Sophronia pointed to the window and subsided to mewling. "Th-there. It's right there."

Behind Lysander, guests were crowding up the steps, the small woman in the brown dress first among them. Lady… Carhill? Cargill?

"If you are intent on disturbing the entire household," Lysander said, "you can at least offer a coherent explanation for your histrionics."

Sophronia waved a hand at the window, though her gaze remained fixed on the carpet. "It's big, and black, and it has legs."

"That description fits my horse."

More guests crowded to the top of the steps, Mrs. Cavanaugh's blue ensemble making her stand out among them. How excellent, how perfectly excellent that Sophronia should mount this drama before the guests the very moment they arrived to Marche Hall.

Lady Cargill sauntered forward. "Oh, look! Somebody is in anticipation of an interesting event."

The statement was so outlandish that even Sophronia peered at the woman. Lysander did too, for the last people he'd willingly welcome under this roof were eccentrics.

"I beg your pardon, my lady?"

She peered at a corner of the window. "Such a conscientious mama the little dears will have. See how perfect the web is."

Lysander lowered his voice. "Madam, what are you going on about?"

"The spider," Sophronia whispered. "The big, black, hairy, *awful*, spider. Right in our front window, Papa."

Lady Cargill took Sophronia's hand. "She loves the light and warmth here, you see. She probably likes to eavesdrop on all the guests as they arrive. She gets to see who is wearing the latest fashions, whose cattle don't match. Spiders are busy creatures, but they do like knowing the latest gossip."

The knot of people at the top of the steps began to dissipate, thank heavens.

Still, this was not an auspicious beginning to the wedding party. "You set up a hue and cry over a mere insect, Sophronia?"

"The spider wasn't there yesterday, Papa. And spiders bite and make sticky webs and they crawl out from under beds."

Now that Lysander's initial terror had subsided, he realized Sophronia was pale, and still whispering. She clung to Lady Cargill's hand, though the woman was a stranger to her.

"Do you know what else spiders do?" Lady Cargill asked. "They really are wonderful in their busy little way."

Spiders made a little crunching sound when a devoted Papa crushed them beneath his boot. Lady Cargill sent Lysander a glance that warned him not to offer that observation.

"What do they do?"

"Well, they have babies, of course. That little ball of nothing is an egg sac, and Madam Spider will defend it with her life, just as your

Papa would defend you with his life. But the truly marvelous thing about spiders is that they gobble up pesky, nasty, flies. I do not care for flies, and horses positively loathe them."

Sophronia darted a gaze at the window. "Spiders *eat* flies?"

The last of the gawking guests, Mrs. Cavanaugh, stood by the newel post through this biology lesson. She sent Lysander an amused, patient look, waggled her fingers at him, and descended to the main hall.

"Spiders must eat something," Lady Cargill went on. "I daresay I am not interested in eating flies, and swatting at them does tire the arm after the first hundred or so."

Outlandish woman, though she'd calmed Sophronia, and turned an awkward situation into a silly moment.

"Sophronia, you will return to the nursery now, please." Lysander said.

"What about the spider, Papa? She's to have a family." Sophronia watched the spider, who was going about her arachnid business oblivious to the upset she'd caused.

How like a female.

Lysander was tempted to scold his daughter. In truth, Sophronia had caused the uproar, though the spider was a rather substantial specimen, and had no business setting up housekeeping in Montmarche's very front window. Then too, Sophronia had been genuinely terrified. Her mother hadn't cared for spiders, and mice would send Maria scrambling onto the nearest stool, bed, or chair.

"We have a full house," Lysander said. "That, that *bug* cannot hatch her family in the Hall when we are already pressed for space. I'll have her taken to the stables, where she can gorge on flies to her heart's content."

"I'm sure she'll appreciate that," Lady Cargill said. "Very well done of you, my lord."

"Papa, do you promise? You won't squash her and leave the babies orphaned?"

He should have predicted that question from Sophronia, but the implications left a sharp ache in his heart. These moments came less and less often, but they hurt all the more for being harder to anticipate.

"The little creatures will have their mama's loving example," he said, "and we will have fewer flies in our stable. I promise."

"There, you see?" Lady Cargill said, smoothing a gloved hand over Sophronia's crown. "All has come right, and you may congratulate yourself on having brought a situation to the attention of the person best placed to solve it. My lord, might you introduce me to your daughter?"

More ridiculousness, for adults did not seek introductions to children, though part of the purpose of house parties was to give young people a chance to try out their manners away from London's ever-judgmental eye.

"Lady Cargill, may I make known to you my daughter, Lady Sophronia Marche. Lady Sophronia, I have the honor to introduce to you Lady Cargill, Viscountess of Cargill."

Sophronia made a pretty little curtsy, which Lady Cargill returned with proper dignity.

"We should name the spider," Sophronia said.

"No, we should not," Lysander said. "We'll be here all day naming the babies, and I'm sure Lady Cargill is wearied from her travels."

Lady Cargill looked to be having a grand time, beaming at the child, who was—thank all the merciful gods—smiling as well.

"She looks like an Octavia to me," Lady Cargill said. "Eight legs, you know. Perhaps we can visit Octavia in the stables tomorrow. For now, she might like some privacy. She must have the maid pack up her dresses for a remove to a better neighborhood and explain the situation to the children."

Sophronia grinned and spun about, making her pinafore bell out, and displaying the grass stain at the back for all to see.

"Octavia, Lady Spider. Please say I may visit the stables with Lady Cargill tomorrow, Papa. We will pay a call on our new friends."

"Do say yes," Lady Cargill echoed. "I love the very scent of a stable, though one isn't supposed to make such an ungenteel admission in polite surrounds."

Lysander loved the scent of the stables. "I see no harm in an outing to the stables, Sophronia, provided other matters are tended to as well." He infused that warning with a bit of sternness, lest all discipline go completely to pot over one spider.

"I must write an essay," Sophronia said, "about how a cigar could have started the Great Fire."

"If you do not scamper off to the nursery this instant," Lysander replied, "I will add an assignment about how children should be neither seen nor heard when guests are arriving."

Sophronia did it again. She pitched herself into him, squeezed hard, then darted off at an unladylike pace. "Yes, Papa. I'm sorry, Papa. I'll write the best essay ever, Papa, and then tomorrow I will *go to the stables with Lady Cargill!*"

She whirled away and darted up the steps at a very unladylike pace.

"I despair of her," Lysander said, rather than attempt to ignore the obvious. "She has a good heart, but her deportment…"

"She's what? Eight or nine?"

"Ten, but small for age. She came a bit early and has never caught up."

Lady Cargill patted his arm. "Plenty of time left for the tutors and governesses to coerce her into conformity, then. You are doubtless very grateful that she's so robust. The children who come early aren't always so lucky. Weak lungs in particular can afflict them sorely."

Coerce her into conformity? Surely her ladyship was speaking metaphorically. But no. The child had been caned, contrary to Lysander's specific orders.

"Sophronia's lungs are quite in working order."

Lady Cargill's laugh was low and pleasant. "True enough. Shall you accompany us on our wander through the stables tomorrow, my lord? Time with your daughter will be at a premium in these next two weeks, and I would not want to steal a moment of it from you."

Her ladyship believed he'd miss the interviews with Sophronia regarding her studies, her misbehaviors, her sad deportment at meals. When Maria had been alive visits to the nursery had figured into every day's schedule. Lysander had forgotten that.

"A visit to the stables with a guest will be a pleasant outing at mid-afternoon. I cannot vouch for Sophronia's ability to keep her clothing clean in such an environment." In any environment, come to that.

"My own hems grow dusty in a stable, but oh, the joy of patting a velvety equine nose, the pleasure of hearing the horses contentedly munch their hay."

She spoke with such affection, Lysander nearly left her to go pet Sindri, though the gelding was impatient with affection when there was hay to be consumed.

"I will meet you in the garden by the fountain at three of the clock tomorrow," he said, offering Lady Cargill his arm at the top of the steps. "And my thanks for your assistance with Sophronia's distress."

"One must deal with spiders. One does so more effectively if they are not objects of terror. I can't stand them, myself."

They reached the bottom of the steps and Lady Cargill dropped his arm. She was a small woman, the first thing he'd noticed about her. Small, plainly dressed. Brown hair, brown eyes. He'd put her age at past forty, a neat sparrow of a female who'd likely become tiny in great old age.

"You made up all that nonsense about the baby spiders and the maid packing the dresses for Sophronia's benefit." And she'd done it so easily, so credibly.

"Lady Sophronia was terrified. I would have told her that King George was afraid of spiders if that would have restored her confidence. Until tomorrow afternoon, my lord."

She curtseyed and strode away, rejoining her daughter and

George, who appeared to be in rapt conversation in the alcove where busts of Plato and Socrates flanked a tall window.

Lysander returned to the front terrace, relieved to find that no new guests had arrived. He took a seat on the bench half-way down the portico and sorted through his thoughts. Something about the encounter with the spider—and Lady Cargill—wanted pondering.

Sophronia had been terrified. Lysander had seen that much, and refrained from castigating his daughter as a result. He'd behaved appropriately as a father, which was a relief. But that comment about restoring Sophronia's confidence…

Did Sophronia lack confidence and if so, was that to be celebrated or lamented? Lysander had no idea, though Maria might have had a useful opinion on the matter. What he did know was that Sophronia had not grinned at him as joyously as she had been grinning when she'd taken her leave of him since he had hired her first governess several years ago.

"You spoke honestly when you said you love even the scent of the stables."

If Lord Montmarche loved the stables, Daphne would not have known it from his actions. He strolled along at her side, his pace never varying. He neither raised his voice to rebuke a stable lad who'd nearly dumped a muck cart at the sight of the earl, nor had he lowered his voice to offer any confiding asides.

He watched Lady Sophronia as if trying to puzzle out a vexing riddle, not like a father stealing an extra half hour with his only daughter.

"I probably turn the same half-puzzled, half-displeased expression on my son," Daphne said, when they'd admired the four foals recently arrived in the mare's barn. The youngsters, being equines, were nimble and sure-footed though only a few weeks old. Watching them gambol in their paddock, then dart back to their mothers' sides, oblivious of the future servitude awaiting them, put Daphne out of sorts.

Or perhaps his lordship's company had done that.

"I hope I behold my offspring with a father's watchful eye," Montmarche replied. "How old is your son."

"Charles is fifteen. Going on fifty some days, going on five others."

The earl paused at the door of the barn, while his daughter scratched a sizeable marmalade tomcat about the ears and chin.

"And what, my lady, about the fifty-year-old male do you find so vexatious?"

"Some fifty-year-old males are charming and wise. On a fifteen-year-old boy, those same qualities are seldom genuine. I lost my Charles when my husband died, though, so I cannot blame the boy for his present disposition."

Sophronia picked up the cat, who bore that indignity tolerantly.

"Lost your son in what sense?"

"To the uncles, who would vex a saint, which I do not pretend to be. Lady Sophronia, who is your new friend?"

"Felix, I think," she said. "He's ever so grand. Do you like cats, Lady Cargill?"

"I like them even better than spiders. They are so agreeable when they purr." Though Daphne refused to acquire a lap cat. Old women made fools of themselves over their house cats, and she was not sufficiently elderly to have earned that privilege.

"How do I get him to purr?" Sophronia asked.

"Give him to me," Montmarche said. "He's getting hair all over your pinafore."

The girl handed over the cat, who had, indeed, left a dusting of orange hair on her clothing.

"A fellow likes to have his shoulders rubbed after a hard day of lolling about in the sun," Montmarche said. He scratched the cat's shoulders, which occasioned more shedding.

Also a stentorian purr.

"I believe you two gentlemen are acquainted," Daphne said.

"I ride nigh daily," Montmarche replied, putting the cat down. "Of course I've crossed paths with the occasional stable cat. Come, I'll introduce you to my horse. Sindri is in the stable across the yard."

The earl's equestrian facilities were laid out in a U shape, with quarters for the grooms and coachmen above the stalls. The base of the U served as the carriage house, while the mare's side was also home to saddle rooms, a harness room, a work room with a snug parlor stove, and space devoted to storing grains and medicinals.

The other leg of the U was for the stallions and geldings, who formed the great bulk of the earl's riding stock. As Daphne admired shoulder angles and praised intelligent eyes—on the horses— Sophronia skipped along at her papa's side. She chattered about how Papa had let her start riding lessons, and she did not have her *very own* pony yet, but perhaps soon, if she was *very, very good*, which she would try *very, very hard* to be...

The underlying note of anxiety in the girl's recitation clouded the joy Daphne felt to be out of doors, as did a niggling worry regarding Charles's whereabouts.

The earl, by contrast, seemed to become less formal the longer he bided among the equines.

"This is Sindri," he said, pausing outside the stall of an enormous black horse. "From his dam side, he inherited size and muscle. From the blood stock on the sire's side, he acquired speed and arrogance."

Another cat had captured Sophronia's attention, a half-grown tortoiseshell who demanded to sniff her visitor thoroughly before allowing any petting.

"Arrogance or confidence?" Daphne asked, reaching a hand to the horse.

He ambled over, as most horses would when not consuming fodder.

"Arrogance, and for good reasons. He'll jump anything I put him to, negotiate any footing, and leave horses half his age in the dust.

He's wily and strong, and he was my greatest consolation when my wife went to her reward."

Sindri had the eye of an older horse, in the sense that the contour of his brow had been deepened by time. His gaze, though, was magisterial and his form magnificent.

"He's a gentleman," Daphne said, as warm horsy breath wafted over her fingers. "The only affection I could tolerate when my husband died was from my mare. She'd wrap me in a neck hug, which I've never seen another horse do to another human. I admit I hugged her back, which occasioned tears on my part. She's getting on now, but we still canter about the park on fine mornings."

What odd confidences could be exchanged in a stable.

"I have many lady's mounts who would suit you, should you wish to ride out."

"If you attempt to put me on a pony, my lord, I will not forgive the slight." Many women rode smaller mounts, though Daphne had never been among them.

"Are you worried for your son?" Now Montmarche lowered his voice.

Daphne wasn't tall enough to reach Sindri's ears, but the horse lowered his head so she could attend to them properly.

"He is fifteen, which is reason enough to worry. He leaves for university in the autumn, and though the uncles allowed as how I could bring him along for this gathering, I truly do feel as if I've long since lost him. He's the titleholder, and he tries to order me about as his uncles do, but it won't wash."

Montmache produced a length of carrot from his pocket and slipped it to the horse. "You refuse to be ordered about?"

"I'm his mother. I brought him into this world wet and squalling. I knew him when he was in dresses, and I would die to keep him safe, but a view of women as servants and handmaids would have appalled his father. It certainly appalls me. The issue is money, of course. I control his funds until he turns twenty-five, but if the uncles can control Charles, then they can also coerce me into surrendering sums at their bidding."

The horse craned his neck to sniff at the earl's pocket.

"Shameless nag." Another lump of carrot met its fate. "I suppose the uncles prevail on the boy to plead their cases to you, and you are loath to put your son in the middle of adult arguments. How many uncles are there?"

"Three. One is kind but spineless, one is merely greedy, the third wishes to be the viscount, but will settle for being the viscount's guardian at large for life, provided the key to the family mint goes with that office."

Daphne did not discuss her situation with near-strangers, but something about Montmarche's demeanor—not quite dull, but certainly self-possessed—made the topic bearable.

"And you control the wealth for another ten years?"

"My brother does in theory, but he supports my decisions in fact. Even when Charles turns twenty-five, my settlements will result in my having more wealth than Charles inherits. That horse would purr for you if he could."

Sindri was now wiggling his lips as the earl scratched his chin.

"Don't be fooled by a few dandified airs. He's as sure-footed by moonlight as most horses are at high noon, and he's never missed a distance to a fence."

Wild rides by moonlight? But then, Montmarche would not wish for half the shire to catch him galloping neck-or-nothing as he tried to outrace grief. Moonlight for madness, daytime for being the earl.

"Charles rides well," Daphne said. "I hope he gets that from me."

"Papa rides well," Sophronia called as the tortoiseshell cat skittered straight up a beam into the rafters.

Sindri spooked to the back of his stall, expression indignant.

"My brave steed is unnerved by a little feline," Montmarche said, taking up a hay fork and serving the horse a snack. "Somebody is overdue for an outing."

Daphne had formed the thought, *I'd enjoy a good gallop*, when

Emma Cavanaugh came around the corner of the stable, her riding habit skirt looped about her wrist. She wore a fetching green ensemble today, and a ridiculous little top hat cocked at a ridiculous angle.

For a woman who'd borne four children, she still had a ridiculously narrow waist, too.

"Mrs. Cavanaugh, good day," Montmarche said, bowing over her gloved hand.

"My lord, my lady, and who is this fine fellow?"

Flirtation ensued, though to his credit Sindri was having none of it. He inhaled his hay, while Mrs. Cavanaugh admired his muscular quarters, his broad shoulders, and all but asked to see his letters patent.

Montmarche made the polite replies, which was, of course, what a proper host should do.

"I'll take Lady Sophronia back to the house with me," Daphne said. "His lordship was just remarking that Sindri could use some exercise and the afternoon is fine, after all."

Emma smiled graciously. "My mare is in exactly the same woeful state, my lord. Do let's have a run together."

The poor mare had likely been either ridden or led a significant distance daily for the past several days, but then, Emma wasn't taking to the saddle to chase a fox.

"A short hack only," Montmarche said. "Lady Cargill, my thanks for your time. I'll see you at dinner." He bowed over Daphne's bare hand, for she'd removed her gloves, the better to pet various beasts. His grip was warm, while her fingers doubtless smelled of horse.

"Until dinner, my lord. Mrs. Cavanaugh. Have a pleasant gallop."

His expression remained unreadable, neither genial nor forbidding. "Perhaps you'd take Sophronia back to the house by way of the small kitchen garden. The herbaceous borders show to good advantage this time of year, and the scents are pleasant."

"I'll show you," Sophronia said. "The walls around the kitchen garden are six feet high, though Papa is two inches taller than that. How do the mice and bunnies get in, if the walls are so high?"

Daphne let herself be led away, while Montmarche called for his gelding to be saddled. Sophronia prattled on about the Great Fire and what if cats smoked cigars—truly, she had a prodigious imagination and an even more impressive vocabulary—until high brick walls appeared around a bend in the path.

"That's the little kitchen garden," Sophronia said. "When I was small, I was allowed to play there, because the walls kept me safe. Everybody was afraid I'd wander into the maze and be lost *forever*. I am my papa's only daughter, and George is his only son. Getting lost in the maze was not allowed, even for George."

And a bereaved earl with one son would of course, look to remarry a woman young enough to bear him another, if he looked to remarry at all. That thought did not signify, and yet, it hurt. Daphne had borne all the children she cared to have—bearing children was dangerous and painful beyond imagining—but did that mean she was no longer female in the eyes of even a man who was himself no longer young?

Pointless question.

"You would not have been lost forever," Daphne said, as an acrid odor assailed her. "Your mama and papa would have come to find you. Depend upon that."

"Something stinks," Sophronia replied, taking Daphne by the hand, and towing her toward an arched door in the high brick wall. The child pushed the door open just as a burst of male laughter sounded from within the garden.

Daphne's mind had just connected the stink and the laughter and the earl's suggestion that she return home by this path when Sophronia darted through the door.

"Cigars," the girl said. "I knew it. Did you fellows steal those from my papa, and may I try one?"

CHAPTER THREE

Emma Cavanaugh was a handsome woman. Eight or ten years ago, she'd doubtless made a stunning debut, and time had been kind to her. Her figure was impressive, she sat a horse tolerably well, and her small talk stayed on the friendly side of gossip.

Sindri didn't like her at all. He pranced and snorted and bucked for good measure, shied at an invisible hedgehog, and jumped the merest rill as if it were the mighty Thames.

All the while, Mrs. Cavanaugh's mare toddled stolidly on, though the poor horse was clearly more in need of a nap than a gallop.

"How do you find your prospective nephew-in-law, my lord?" Mrs. Cavanaugh asked as they ambled down a leafy bridle path. "I cannot say I'm well acquainted with him."

Why should she be? "Prescott is a fine young man, or he'd not be allowed to so much as glance at Helena's hems."

Mrs. Cavanaugh stroked her glove down the mare's glossy neck. "He and Miss Gavineau aren't a love match? So refreshing, to find young people willing to take a sensible approach to marriage. Both of my husbands were sensible men, and our unions were cordial and pleasing to all involved."

That was plain speaking, which Lysander should have appreciated. "Helena and her swain are devoted, though they are quiet about it. I'm sure they'll be happy."

Until one of them died, and then the other would be left to race about the shire after dark, which admission Lysander had had no business making to Lady Cargill. She'd confessed to hugging her mare though, and *only* her mare.

"Marriage is a happy estate, is it not?" Mrs. Cavanaugh said. "I much prefer it to the freedoms a widow has. It isn't good for a man to be alone, and one must conclude that Scripture implies woman does not prosper easily in the unwed state either. What a beautiful property you have."

They'd ridden a path along the perimeter of the park, one Sindri usually took at a dead run. "Thank you. I was fortunate to inherit from a man who took his responsibilities seriously. Where do you bide when you're not in Town?"

He ought to know. She was a suitable candidate to become his next countess, and details, such as where her sons' properties were, merited investigation.

"Here and there," she said, stroking her mare's shoulder this time. "My family holds land in Surrey and Kent, my boys have properties in Sussex and Hampshire, though of course, those are managed by our factors. Is Marche Hall your largest holding, my lord?"

Sindri shied at a falling leaf.

"Marche Hall is the oldest and largest of my holdings. My horse is in a fractious mood today. Rather than impose on you any longer, I'll escort you to the stables. His temper tends to deteriorate once he's reached the limit of his patience."

"High spirits in a healthy male specimen are to be expected," she said. "We ladies know to bide our time and wait for a more obliging mood from our escorts."

Her flirtation was not the giggling, frothy annoyance Lysander endured from very young women, and it wasn't the hard-eyed pursuit the courtesans turned in his direction when they sought a new protector. Mrs. Cavanaugh was something in between, determined without being undignified. A little self-mocking, a little desperate.

And Lysander was more than a little annoyed, which was unfair of him. In his day, men did the pursuing, and the ladies did the choosing. Too set in his ways, as his sister Cassandra had often said.

Mrs. Cavanaugh discussed the activities planned for the next two weeks—Cassandra, as mother of the bride, had all in hand, as usual—and Mrs. Cavanaugh offered repeatedly to assist in any capacity.

Lysander needed no assistance.

Except with Sophronia, whom Mrs. Cavanaugh had mentioned not even once.

Lady Cargill, by contrast, had explained to Sophronia that in the vast bounds of the stable, Octavia, Lady Spider, would have found many ideal places to set up housekeeping. Lady Cargill had held hands with the girl, a familiarity Lysander had stopped indulging in two years ago.

Lady Cargill had also admitted to crying on her mare's shoulder, and Sindri had taken to her ladyship on the spot—not that a cork-brained gelding was a good judge of who should become the next Countess of Montmarche.

And not that Lysander was considering a contrary, outspoken little widow of a certain age for that office anyhow.

Do not embarrass your son. Do not embarrass your son again.

"Mr. Offenbach, Charles, good afternoon."

Sophronia, bless the girl, had gone silent beside Daphne. The stink of lit cigars violated the otherwise lovely fragrance of the garden. Thirty yards away, maids worked by the opposite wall, gathering vegetables for the enormous evening meal already in preparation for the guests.

"Mama." Charles held a cigar, smoke trailing from the tip. He was as pale as the full moon, while Mr. Offenbach exuded the confident air of an aspiring rakehell.

"My lady." Offenbach swept a bow, leaving a trail of smoke from his cheroot. "We ought not to be smoking in proximity to food stuffs, but the urge overtook us as we strolled the formal garden."

Which did not explain why hiding behind the walls of the kitchen garden had been necessary.

"The grounds here are lovely," Daphne said. "Do you gentlemen know Lady Sophronia Marche?"

To his credit, Charles offered the girl a bow. "My lady. Cargill, at your service." He sounded exactly like his father, and even his bow was reminiscent of the late viscount. Charles was growing into his father's height too, thank heavens, though he still had a boy's slenderness and schoolroom pallor.

Offenbach cast his cigar into a row of staked beans. "Mr. Absalom Offenbach. Pleased to make your acquaintance, my lady."

Sophronia dipped a curtsey. "You should not have pitched that cigar anywhere without making sure it was no longer lit, Mr. Offenbach. Fires can start from a mere spark."

Good for you. "She's right," Daphne added, because Offenbach's response was to adjust the lace at his cuffs and look amused.

Charles strode down the row of beans. "Can't say *haricots verts au cigare* would be to my taste." He plucked the smoking cigar from the ground "Will I see you at dinner, Mama?"

Asked a bit too cheerfully.

"Of course, which means I'd best be getting back to the house. Where is your room, Charles?"

Offenbach was positively smirking at that question. "His lordship and I are sharing quarters. We're in the bachelor wing, on the family side of the house one floor below Montmarche's suite. Fine view of the stables and grounds. Any footman can get word to us if your ladyship should have need of your son."

What a supercilious, boorish, self-important young man. "If I require my son's company, Mr. Offenbach, I will not send a footman to fetch him for an interview, as if he were a tenant behind on the rent. Good day."

Lady Sophronia gave the cigars in Charles's hands a brooding look and darted through the garden door.

"Why are men like that?" she asked. "All mean and nasty. Lord Cargill seems like a nice enough sort, but I do not care for Mr. Offenbach. He pitched a *lit cigar* into Papa's garden."

Sophronia's voice doubtless carried over the garden wall. Daphne made sure hers did as well.

"Young men, particularly young men of no consequence, sometimes try to puff themselves up with arrogance because they have nothing of value to offer the world. They refuse the hard work of learning a trade, they disdain the education made available to them at university, so they idle about, trying vainly to turn sport, fashion, and leisure into gentlemanly pursuits. We should pity them."

Though Daphne did not pity Mr. Offenbach. He'd been dressed in the height of gentlemanly elegance, right down to the lace brushing his knuckles. He had "bad influence" written all over him, and was just the sort of company Charles should avoid.

"Do we have time to take the path through the woods?" Sophronia asked.

They'd taken a wandering, leisurely stroll from the stables, the fresh air doing much to revive Daphne's spirits. "We have at least an hour before anybody has to dress for dinner. Why?"

"The maze is that way." Sophronia gestured toward a hedgerow of elms. "We walk past it on the way to the woods. The maze is out of sight of the house, except for a corner of the east wing, which makes it more confusing. You can barely see anything but hedges when you're in the maze. I'm not to go there by myself."

Daphne had been allowed a generous portion of solitude as a child. She'd read in the hayloft, built rock dams in streams, turned climbing trees into ships of the line, and held garden tea parties with her dolls.

"Is it a large maze?"

"One of the largest in the realm. Papa told George we should cut the damned thing down and put up a glass house, but George says the maze is a family legacy, and we must preserve it for future generations."

Daphne paused with the girl where a laburnum alley intersected with the walking path. "What do you think?"

Sophronia's brows, dark like her father's, drew down making a resemblance to her sire apparent. "What do I think?"

"Surely you have an opinion?" Though being raised as a female in a titled household, she was likely being taught *not* to have opinions. She was to have small talk, manners, and eventually, children. Phoebe was a product of such an upbringing, and Daphne regretted that.

The laburnum was long past blooming, so the arching branches made an alley of greenery and shade. Benches had been placed at intervals, and a tall privet hedge rose at the end.

"I think Papa worries about keeping up with progress," Sophronia said, "while George wants to be thought respectful of the past. Nobody needs a maze, Papa says, but then, nobody needs fairytales either."

Were those her father's words? "I need fairytales. They inspire me to slay dragons and go on quests. Let's sit for a moment, shall we?"

Sophronia skipped to a bench and took a seat, smoothing her skirts with unconscious grace. "You are being silly, which is kind of you. I like you."

Oh, child... Affection should not be so easily given. "I am not being silly at all. I am merely the niece of a baron from Shropshire, and should not have made any sort of come out, except that my aunt wanted company for one of my cousins. I was sent off to London, equipped with a wardrobe, and given cursory instruction from my cousin's finishing governess. I faced many dragons, Sophronia, and they would have dined on my bones if I'd let them."

"But you didn't let them. You are a viscountess now. Mrs. Cavanaugh is a dragon. She wants to dine on Papa's bones."

Daphne saw no point dissembling in the face of that truth. "Mrs. Cavanaugh is actually quite nice. She has four sons, and if she made your Papa happy, then you would benefit from her ambition."

Sophronia heaved up a sigh the size of Shropshire. "That's what George says. He says I'm not to worry over gaining a step-mama, because I will go to school when I'm fourteen and marry after I make my come out, but if I don't worry over Papa, who will? He's very serious, and I won't be fourteen for ages and ages."

"That a grown man takes life seriously is an appealing quality." Though Montmarche did not seem to take *himself* too seriously, another appealing quality. "Shall we have a peek at the maze?"

"We can peek," Sophronia replied, bolting from the bench, "but we're not to go inside. Papa has a rule."

A man in homespun attire occupied a chair where the hedge opened into the maze. He rose and bowed. "Ladies, good day."

"Good day, Mr. Perkins," Sophronia said. "This is Lady Cargill. I wanted to show her the maze."

"From the outside," Daphne added. The hedges were twelve feet tall at least, and the growth impenetrably thick. A rabbit might be able to wiggle through the hedges, a person could not. "I understand guests are to avoid the maze."

"The guests, the servants, even the groundskeepers stay clear unless we're trimmin' the hedges. His lordship's orders. One of the largest mazes in England, you see. Easy to get lost."

He was not simply proud of his maze, he was respectful of it. Daphne gave the towering greenery an uneasy glance. Why would anybody devote such effort to a place where the most likely outcome was to lose one's bearings?

"Is there a rule for navigating the maze?"

Perkins smiled. "It's a secret passed down from earl to earl. Lord Killoway should have learned the secret on his twenty-first birthday."

"George is Lord Killoway," Sophronia said. "He doesn't like to use the title at home. He promised to tell me the secret when I turn one and twenty."

Daphne was coming to like Montmarche's son, and she'd barely been introduced to him. "Let's have a ramble through the woods, then, shall we? After spending days in a coach, I'm not quite ready to go back into the house yet."

Through the trees she caught a glimpse of Montmarche and Mrs. Cavanaugh trotting along the edge of the park. The widow cut a lovely figure in her fashionable green habit.

Daphne turned toward the woods rather than watch Montmarche assist the lady from her horse. Emma Cavanaugh would make the most of that moment, while Daphne wanted to make the most of what fresh air she could enjoy before being forced to make inane conversation for hours at dinner.

∼

"A buffet was a wise choice for the first evening," Lysander said. "You've given our guests a chance to mingle without the regimentation of a seating order."

The anxiety in Cassandra's gaze eased as she surveyed the guests ranged around the parlors. The informal parlor, the first formal parlor and the music room stretched in one continuous space by virtue of open folding doors.

The doors to the back terrace had similarly been flung wide, meaning a party of more than thirty could spread out enough for private conversation, but remain gathered enough that wandering and regrouping between trips to the buffet was easy.

"We will have plenty of dinners before the guests disperse," Cassandra said. "A buffet is easier on both the staff and the guests, though some people need the pre-arranged seating order. Otherwise, they will sit in the corner with their school friends and neighbors from back home, never venturing to speak to more recent acquaintances."

Lysander's job had been to welcome each new arrival and see

them settled. Cassandra bore the brunt of most of the introductions, which she'd been making as the day had progressed.

"What's the Offenbach whelp doing here? He's been sent down from university twice, and from what I recall, his prospects are limited."

Offenbach was an extra spare without portfolio, not a comfortable status. He was good-looking, well-dressed, and held membership in a modest club, but Lysander had reason to know the man was slow to pay his vowels and had engaged in two duels in the past six months.

"He's the bad example," Cassandra said, taking a sip of raspberry lemonade punch. "He's the fellow the young ladies might end up with if they don't accept more promising offers. He's good for making up numbers, he's competent on the dance floor, and he doesn't cheat at cards. He'll do for my purposes."

"Never underestimate woman's capacity for strategy."

Cassandra's smile reminded Lysander of the girl she'd been. "You quote Papa."

"Who quoted Mama. I suppose George is the good example?" Lysander's son had acquitted himself well as understudy to the host. He'd welcomed guests, known most everybody's name before they'd left their carriages, and shown the young men to their quarters.

The fluttering young ladies had inspired George to genial banter, nothing more. His mama would have been proud of him.

"George needs to marry sooner rather than later," Cassandra said, smile fading. "We've had that discussion, Montmarche."

Many times. "He's barely reached his majority, my dear. Give him a few years to kick up his heels before he takes on the burden of a wife and children. I had that privilege, and made a better choice when I did marry my countess."

"You have no spare, my lord. You are getting on, George has no cousins through the Marche line. We have no younger siblings. Unless you want some American backwoodsman to inherit the title, either you or George should be marrying and having sons."

Getting on. Cassandra's tactics were shifting, from wheedling and hinting to outright insults.

"Let's enjoy the terrace, shall we?" Where a brother and sister could speak honestly.

Cassandra took his arm. "You are fifty years old, sir. While you remain a vigorous exponent of your gender, many men don't see even that many years on earth. Three score and ten is for the few and the lucky."

They crossed onto the terrace, the fresh air and quiet welcome. "Cassandra, I know."

"If you know, and you realize that securing the succession with a spare is one way to ensure that George needn't hurry into marriage, then why haven't you taken another bride, Montmarche? Must I explain the details to you?"

She had been such a comfort to him in the years after Maria's death. Sophronia's French was fluent already because Cassandra and her husband, Amery Gavineau, had invited their niece for extended holidays with them in Nice and Paris. Sophronia knew the sights of both Paris and London thanks to her aunt, and had acquaintans on both sides of the Channel.

Never a bad thing, for an earl's daughter.

"I well understand the details of procreation, madam."

"Are you in love with an unsuitable *parti*, is that it? You are old enough that you could get away with marrying a mistress, provided she was somewhat decent. A merry widow, a cit, an opera singer from the Continent. People would understand that an older man needs the comfort of a wife in his declining years, and you can afford to be selfish about your choice."

They wandered down the steps into the formal parterres that Lysander's grandmother had so treasured. She had been French, as Gavineau was French, and had disdained the English craze for creating a caricature of nature at great effort and expense. She was the reason the park stretching before the house yet flourished without artificial landscaping.

"If I take another wife, she will be a suitable *parti*, for she might well have the raising of the next earl, or of George's heir."

"You are considering it? Remarrying, that is?"

The gravel crunched beneath Lysander's boots, his steps disturbing the pattern that had been carefully raked into the walkway. Tomorrow, before the sun rose, the pattern would be restored by the labor of the gardeners and grooms.

Everybody pitched in during a house party, the lines between house and grounds, stable and home farm, blurring in an effort to offer the best hospitality Marche Hall could shower upon its guests.

"I have considered remarrying since I put off mourning. I am well aware that I have only the one son. I hadn't thought through as carefully how the lack of a spare burdens George."

Lysander's firstborn was perched on the balustrade, young ladies on a bench beside him. A gangling sprig bracketed the bench attempting the same easy posture as George, but that fellow was younger and less assured. Offenbach had taken the end of the bench, crowding the young ladies, though they seemed pleased to have his company.

"It's not as if having a spare involves the labors of Hercules, not for you," Cassandra said. "Your countess will be the one giving birth, after all."

But Lysander would be the papa. He didn't dread that, exactly, but neither did he look forward to it. Children, viewed from any informed perspective, were a terrifying prospect. Children with a woman other than Maria were... expedient. Necessary. Duty.

No child should be conceived strictly as a concession to duty.

"Have you chosen a countess for me?" The question was only half in jest.

"I would never be so bold, though you will find among the guests several women of appropriate age and station to fulfill that office."

The young people burst into laughter as Offenbach rose, handkerchief in hand, to dab at the young sprig's cravat. A splash of claret decorated the youth's linen, and his face had turned nearly the same color as the stain.

"I must intervene," Lysander said. "Offenbach is making sport of another guest."

"It was an accident," Cassandra said, keeping hold of Lysander's elbow. "George will prevent them from coming to blows. You can only create greater awkwardness."

The slender young fellow bowed to the ladies and left the group, marching across the terrace with an air of injured dignity.

"The problem with having a bad example on hand is that he'll live down to the role in which he was cast."

"Meaning," Cassandra replied, turning Lysander back toward the terrace. "George will make a very fine good example, won't he?"

George did not need the contrast a bad example provided. He was a son a father could be proud of, an heir more than worthy of the title.

"Then you've recruited potential countesses among the guests," Lysander said. "Do I take it Mrs. Cavanaugh is the good example?"

"She is comely, sensible, young enough but not too young, and has had *four sons*, all of whom appear to be thriving."

A summary worthy of the auctioneer at Tatts. "Is there a bad example among the ladies?"

"Of course not. My daughter's wedding party is a gathering of fine company, and every lady present is above reproach. If there's an older widow or a spinster among the guests, that's by happenstance."

Never underestimate the strategy of women.

"No, it isn't." The lone older widow on the premises was Lady Cargill, who'd apparently had only a daughter and one son, was past her child-bearing years or nearly so, rather plain, and given to rescuing spiders.

Not very subtle, but then, Lysander was *getting on* and Cassandra was nothing, if not determined that he should remarry.

"Oh, there's Mrs. Cavanaugh sitting all by herself," Cassandra said, though Mrs. Cavanaugh was on the terrace, and somebody else would doubtless soon occupy the half of the bench she'd left empty. "Why don't you be a proper host and find her some company?"

Lysander passed his sister his drink. "Subtle, Cassandra. Very subtle."

She poured his drink into her own. "All I'm asking you to do is keep an open mind."

She was asking him to surrender his freedom, sire a child or three, and replace Maria with another countess.

"I'll find the lady some company, then get myself more punch." He plucked the empty glass from her hand, and prepared to be a proper host.

Again.

CHAPTER FOUR

"I am awful," Daphne announced to the headstones dotting a neatly trimmed square of grass. "Two days into this house party, and I want to leave. No reflection on present company."

Sophronia had shown her the family plot, another feature sheltered within the rambling wood. A grotto, a folly, a fishing cottage, and many walking paths were tucked beneath a mature forest, and on its edge sat an ancient chapel and this cemetery.

Some of the headstones were no longer legible, two were recent, as headstones went, one large and one less imposing. A hard bench sat along the wrought iron fencing, and sunshine gave the place a peaceful feeling. A pair of common blue butterflies flitted about the smaller headstone, one lighting for a moment then dancing away.

"You talk to the departed," a male voice said.

Montmarche stood at the edge of the trees. He wore riding attire again, and blunt spurs on his boots. "Am I interrupting?"

Daphne had watched him the previous evening, circulating among the guests, moving easily from room to room and from house to terrace. He was entirely at home in the role of host, never tarrying too long with any person, occasionally adding a guest to one group, or drawing a guest away for a moment of conversation.

He'd taken Mrs. Cavanaugh for a stroll through the gardens, though what was there to see about formal parterres, privet hedges, and urns full of petunias?

"I talk to the departed," Daphne said, "and to butterflies. Of course you may join me. Your family lies here."

He let himself through the gate and took the place beside her. "I pay my respects often, and then the mood leaves me and I don't feel so inclined for weeks at a time. Then I'm back again, burdening poor Maria with my every woe and regret. She was endlessly patient with me in life, and she adored the butterflies. Said there was nothing common about the common blue."

He missed his wife. That he admitted as much made him more human, less an aristocrat.

"James loved the butterflies as well. They'd pay their respects to him whenever he read in the garden," Daphne said. "I talk to him too, mostly about the children. He was a conscientious father, though I ought to have argued harder for my offspring. The uncles forbade me to address a departed spouse in the children's hearing."

Montmarche set his hat on the bench and ran his hand through his hair. "Whyever should a man's brothers forbid his widow from harmless behavior common to the bereaved?"

"They would like to have me declared an unfit parent. They would have sent Charles off to public school within weeks of James's death, but James's will specifically forbid such behavior until Charles was twelve. I still think it was too soon."

Montmarche sat forward bracing his elbows on his knees. He shot a scowl at Daphne over his shoulder.

"The uncles want to control the children's funds," he said. "They are apparently not even subtle about that objective."

"They want to control *all* the funds," Daphne said. "Thank heavens I have a brother willing to stand up to the uncles, though even he can't stop them from meddling."

"How can they get to your settlements?"

This was not a conversation to have with a near stranger, but Montmarche was a peer. He understood issues of inheritance and family intrigue, and he was asking Daphne to provide the details when he might well have changed the topic.

"The uncles—Mr. Terrance Cargill in particular—can show the courts that my brother has failed to exercise good judgment where I'm concerned, that I'm reckless and immoral. The usual slights hurled at women who think for themselves."

"You think for yourself?" Montmarche regarded her with convincing gravity. "We can't have you inspiring other ladies to domestic revolt, can we? Husbands might have to listen to their wives for a change and the realm would topple."

He had a house full of guests, and yet, he'd sought the consolation of his wife's graveside. "You listened to your countess. You solicited her advice, and you seek it still. You are teasing me."

His smile was more charming for illuminating a sober countenance. "Guilty as charged. My sister has set notions about what this gathering is to accomplish, and I am to play the role assigned to me—a sensible role, but not one I auditioned for. How are you finding the company so far?"

That was a faultlessly executed change of topic. Daphne's grasping in-laws hadn't put him off, but a mention of old grief had.

"I find the company congenial," Daphne said. "The young people are getting along, and they are the usual source of drama at such gatherings. I am somewhat concerned for Charles. Some fool has—he's been billeted with Mr. Absalom Offenbach, and I dislike what I've seen of that gentleman's deportment."

Montmarche sat up and rested his arm along the back of the bench. "I'm told Mr. Offenbach is the cautionary tale."

"I beg your pardon?"

"He's the stylish young swell who hasn't a feather to fly with. His life will be one of making up the numbers, idling about his club, and avoiding creditors. He's good-looking, lazy, and entirely self-interested. Unless he marries an heiress or settles to a profession, he's likely to end up in disgrace."

Montmarche's arm was not around Daphne's shoulders, but his pose was casual. He either did not care for propriety as much as his formal mannerisms suggested, or in this place, he set propriety aside from long habit.

Did he ever cuddle with anybody? Hug his horse? His daughter? A favorite hound? Montmarche looked like a man with no use for simple affection, but he clearly loved his daughter, spoiled his horse, and missed his wife.

Daphne loosened the ribbons of her bonnet and set it next to Montmarche's hat. "I wish whoever had done the sleeping arrangements hadn't put Charles in the same room with Mr. Offenbach. Charles has weathered a few years at public school, but Offenbach is an order of magnitude more wicked than a schoolyard scoundrel."

"Offenbach doubtless *was* the schoolyard scoundrel. I'll keep an eye on Lord Cargill, if you like. A host ought to be mindful of his guests."

The offer was casual, though Montmarche would keep his word.

"I'd appreciate that. A mother is a nuisance to a boy of fifteen, particularly to a boy with a title and an expectation of wealth and responsibility."

His lordship rose and offered Daphne his hand. "I beg to differ, having watched my son come of age without the benefit of his mother's guidance. A mama can explain things a papa cannot, things one's school chums hold forth about endlessly, from a position of vast ignorance. What do young ladies truly want? Do women really care nothing for a man's appearance so long as he's jolly and reliable? How does a fellow know a lady will be receptive to his kisses? All manner of mysteries lie within a mother's power to unlock."

Daphne took his hand and linked arms with him, looping her bonnet over her wrist. "Whereas a Papa's job is to simply be there, setting an example of how a young lady should expect to be treated. I cannot imagine Phoebe ever asking her father what young men truly want, or what his answer would have been."

Montmarche held the gate open for Daphne, then offered his arm. "Heaven knows, the young men have an answer for that one. A pack of rutting fools the lot of them."

"Were you a rutting fool?" She took his arm for the sheer pleasure of touching a healthy male on a pretty day.

"Oh, quite. My father took me aside, explained the rules to me, and increased my allowance by an amount that allowed me to limit my frolicking to those parties who played the game by the same guidelines. I did not seek a wife until I'd grown bored with the whole business of being an heir about Town. I fear George won't have the same luxury."

"Viscount Killoway."

The earl led her down the path that wound through the woods, where dappled shade and deep quiet created a fairytale setting for butterflies playing in sunbeams. He owned these woods, and thank heavens he had the wisdom to appreciate them.

"George only began using the title at university. Sophronia always calls him George, and the staff has been reluctant to apply the courtesy title to him."

"Then you must set the example, my lord. Your son is of age, any day he might have to step into your shoes, and a courtesy title is a reminder of that possibility."

Montmarche on first impression had an air of impatience, whether greeting guests, scolding his daughter, or in conversation. In the stables and in the woods, he was more relaxed. His pace was leisurely, his words measured.

"I suppose I don't want him to grow up. Bad of me."

"Human of you. Phoebe wails constantly about not having found a spouse yet, but ye gods. Why would any young woman be so desperate to take on the risks of childbed? Are a man's affections worth dying for? Is spinsterhood really a fate worse than death? I loved my husband, but this desperation we visit upon our young women to marry anybody in breeches... I'm sorry."

He regarded her from down the length of his nose as if she'd suggested Napoleon wasn't a bad sort, except for that little business of causing several million deaths.

"I nearly died," Daphne said, "with Charles. He was not in the correct position to be born, and the physician could only admonish me to try harder. If my sister-in-law hadn't sent for a French midwife, I'd be dead, and all Phoebe wants, all she longs for—"

Daphne would have dashed off into the undergrowth to rant at the trees, but Montmarche covered her hand with his own.

"We lost a child," he said. "Between George and Sophronia. She lived a few days, but was not robust. Like Sophronia, she came early. I nearly lost my wife to the grief."

He spoke quietly, as if he stood with Daphne not amid towering oaks, but in a chapel.

She stepped closer, wrapping her arms around him, and he enfolded her in an embrace. Of all people, of all men, Daphne would not have envisioned herself in Montmarche's arms, but he knew how to share comfort, how to hold a woman so she could gain some purchase on unsettled nerves and a weary heart.

"It's terrifying, isn't it?" Montmarche said. "Raising children. Bad enough when their other parent shares the upheaval and drama with you. Far worse, when you must soldier on alone. And then they grow up, and *alone* acquires new and daunting dimensions."

He smelled good, of lemon and mint, such as the French might blend into a hard soap. He was warm too, and solidly muscular. Daphne let herself notice no more than that before she stepped back. She was a woman well past youth, and hadn't *noticed* a man in any personal sense for years.

"Exactly, my lord. When the children are small, we worry about runaway coaches and putrid sore throats, because all manner of bad fates can lay a child low. Then they grow up, and we're to stand back, letting a cruel and dangerous world strike blow after blow while we wave our handkerchiefs and pretend adulthood is a great lark."

He looked around at the trees. "Some of adulthood should be a lark. One loses sight of that. One cannot always be minding one's duty. I still occasionally ride hellbent across my acres. What of you? What is your version of a lark?"

Certainly not loitering in a forest while imposing on a man's kind-heartedness. "I paint. Mostly, I tromp around, pretending to be searching for an ideal vantage point from which to render a landscape, but in truth, I'm simply enjoying the out of doors."

He offered his arm again, and Daphne took it. "Then for the duration of your visit to Marche Hall, you must tromp wherever you please, my lady. Consider the estate your canvas, and I will make your excuses to the other guests. George is something of an amateur artist, so don't be surprised if he asks to tromp with you."

"I'm sure, if he's like his father, he'll be very good company."

This occasioned another one of those subtle, attractive smiles, though Daphne had offered the plain truth. Lord Montmarche wasn't silly, vain, self-absorbed, or any of a thousand other pejoratives she could apply to most of the titled men whose company she'd kept.

He turned the discussion to the bride and groom, and the arrangements being made for the formal ball that would follow the wedding. Daphne argued for putting three waltzes on the program, his lordship wanted none, but was prepared to graciously allow one in honor of the happy couple.

They emerged from the woods near the laburnum alley, and Montmarche bowed over Daphne's hand.

"Please excuse me, Lady Cargill. If I attempt to visit the stables without stopping by the conservatory, my sister, who is choosing flowers for tonight's centerpiece, will force me to play duets in public. I have much enjoyed our walk."

They were not yet in sight of the house, but Emma Cavanaugh

sat in plain view on a bench nearer to the maze. She was reading, or pretending to.

"I have enjoyed our ramble as well, my lord. Thank you for your escort, and as for Viscount Killoway's question..."

Montmarche looked puzzled.

"How does a fellow know if a lady is willing to be kissed? That one's easy." Daphne offered a curtsey and tossed her answer over her shoulder. "He asks her for her opinion on the matter." She strode away in the direction of the house, swinging her bonnet by its ribbons.

∼

"But lilies do last quite well," Mrs. Cavanaugh said, "and in yellow and pink, they carry no mournful message."

"The blooms are large though," Cassandra countered. "We want low centerpieces for our evening meal, because we will not be strictly formal, not until Sunday."

"Perhaps little pots of heartsease," Mrs. Cavanaugh suggested. "They are so cheerful. No fragrance will compete with enjoyment of the food, and they aren't the usual thing."

Lysander's head gardener stood a few respectful paces back while the ladies sparred, for as determined as Mrs. Cavanaugh was to be helpful, Cassandra was equally determined to maintain her authority as hostess, sister to the earl, and mother of the bride.

The ladies held this discussion not in the ornamental portion of the conservatory, but in the functional expanse of the glass house. The scent here was rich earth and greenery, the air warm and humid.

"I favor the notion of heartsease," Lysander said, mostly because his gardener had work to do, and Lysander would rather be anywhere else. "A bit of novelty about the table setting, some informality, will establish the tone for our first dinner nicely. Excellent suggestion, Mrs. Cavanaugh."

Both women beamed at him, and abruptly, Lysander realized what the point of the digression had been. Emma Cavanaugh had been colluding with Cassandra rather than in conflict with her, and Lysander had fallen into their ambush.

Lysander's father had explained much parliamentary strategy to him. One of the first tenets of winning support from a man reluctant to surrender his vote was to get that man to capitulate on some small, unrelated matter—the wine pairing at a club dinner, the bridle path chosen for a companionable morning hack, whether or not to switch out a deck of cards mid-way through the evening.

Small concessions led to a subtle shift in perspective, and that led to a change of behavior.

Lysander had made a concession by supporting Emma Cavanaugh's heartsease.

The gardener cleared his throat. "I'll have the centerpieces set out for the footmen by five of the clock, shall I?"

Mrs. Cavanaugh curled her hand around Lysander's arm. "Four would suit. I understand we're keeping country hours through the week."

"I'm so glad that's settled," Cassandra said, her comment bearing portents beyond a mere choice of flowers. "I'll see you at luncheon, my lord, Mrs. Cavanaugh. Perhaps Mrs. Cavanaugh might enjoy a tour of the maze, Montmarche."

Perhaps Lysander would like to pitch his sister into the maze and leave her to wander for the next two weeks.

"I'd like nothing better than to enjoy the maze at some length," he said, "but alas, other duties call. If I'm to host dinner and attend my guests this evening, I'd best spend the afternoon in the dull pursuits of a country landowner, which means I must meet with my stablemaster now. Ladies, you will excuse me."

He bowed and strode off, leaving the women to weave marriage spells, or whatever dark magic they pleased. Lysander had not lied—correspondence waited for no earl, and a consultation regarding the stabling of the guests' horses was imperative—but he was being ungracious and that was bad of him.

Bad of him, *again*. He was apparently in a contrary mood today. He walked past a knot of Helena's young friends by the garden fountain and offered them a mere nod—they had no business flirting with him when George was on hand to be flirted with—and continued on until he'd reached the stables.

"I can saddle Sindri myself," Lysander said as a groom greeted him. "You lot have enough to do."

He in fact simply wanted the horse's company.

"Yes, my lord," the groom replied, tugging a forelock, "but perhaps my lord would permit me to fetch the brushes and whatnot?"

The lad was graying, wiry, and had worked on the estate as far back as Lysander could recall. "Mercer, what's afoot? You taught me how to saddle a mount, and you'll teach Lady Sophronia how to saddle hers. I know how to use a curry comb."

Mercer looked up and down the barn aisle, which was spotless, for a barn. Sindri was peering over his half-door, ever one to collect gossip—and carrots.

"The saddle room is in use, my lord."

What the damned devil? "A saddle room is always in use, keeping the gear dry, organized, and safe from thieves. What aren't you saying?"

Mercer took a step closer. "The young swell with the flashy"—Mercer gestured to his throat—"with all the lace. He's helping a lady choose her saddle."

"A lady?" Behind a closed door with the designated-young-rake?

"I'm sure I could not say which lady, my lord, but she had a distinctive laugh."

Mrs. Ingersoll. Her laugh was as distinctive as an ill-fitting boot on a gouty toe. She'd brought two daughters to the gathering and no husband, though Lysander knew for a fact she had one.

"You are saying I'm to be denied my gallop because Mr. Offenbach has chosen to go a-rutting in my stables? Sindri will soon become unmanageable."

Mercer grinned. "I would never impugn my lord's guests with such careless talk, but I warrant Mr. Off-with-his-breeches won't be in there long. He chose another lady's saddle in less than fifteen minutes before breakfast. The lads say we should start timing him, lay a few bets."

Lady Cargill had spotted Offenbach for the boor he was, would that Cassandra had been as discerning.

"Disturb the proceedings, please. Knock loudly, explain that my lordship is underfoot yelling for my horse, and then count to ten before intruding."

"Your lordship isn't yelling," Mercer replied. "Your lordship stopped yelling before you was sent off to public school, more's the pity. Master George gave up yelling at the same sorry pass."

Lord Killoway. "Go," Lysander said, pointing to the saddle room's closed door. "*Now.*" He did not raise his voice, though he wanted to, and not only because Offenbach was being indiscreet.

Lysander chose a corner of the stable yard where he could loiter in the shade with Galahad, the orange tom, until Offenbach and Mrs. Ingersoll strolled out of the stables. Offenbach's cravat was wrinkled, his hair mussed. The lady was not wearing a habit—easier to get under her skirts that way—and Offenbach was smirking.

Lysander kept his peace while they passed him, oblivious to his presence.

Lady Cargill's earlier comment came back to him: The second day of the gathering, and she had wanted to leave. That remark had soured Lysander's mood, though given Offenbach's behavior, he not only understood her sentiment, he shared it.

Offenbach was a problem, Mrs. Cavanaugh was a problem—also a potential solution—and that moment stolen with Lady Cargill in the woods was also, in a way Lysander didn't want to examine, a problem.

He set the cat aside and strode into the stables, yelling for his horse.

~

"Perishing bloody nonsense, keeping country hours," Offenbach said, wrapping another length of starched linen around his throat. Five discards were draped over the wardrobe's open door, like so many barber's bandages minus the blood. "How can a fellow enjoy himself when the livelong evening must be spent in company?"

Charles had been fascinated to observe the great dandy tying his own neckcloth the first three times that honor had befallen him. By the sixth rendition of the ritual, he was bored. The last two discards had been merely for the pleasure of aggravating the Montmarche servants, who were tending to Offenbach's laundry along with their many other duties.

"I thought good company *was* how a fellow enjoyed himself," Charles said. "You seemed to delight in Mrs. Ingersoll's company on the way to the stables."

Charles had recalled a pressing obligation to rehearse with his sister in the music room the moment Mrs. Ingersoll had let go with a certain laugh. That laugh had been merry, but also naughty. Phoebe could be counted on to back a fellow up and without asking questions, so Charles had spent an entire fifteen minutes with her choosing music they'd likely never perform.

Though he liked accompanying his sister. He hadn't had that privilege since being shooed off to public school.

"Noticed Mrs. Ingersoll's friendly nature did you?" Offenbach said, straightening to admire himself in the cheval mirror. "She might enjoy a romp with a lad new to his pleasures."

Charles had yet to experience those pleasures, but he wasn't about to undertake any romping with Mrs. Ingersoll.

"Poaching on another man's preserves involves risk to a lady's good name and the poacher's continued existence." Charles regretted the words the moment they came out of his mouth. His father might have said something like this. His mother had been less delicate. *Don't be so stupid as to get called out over somebody's errant wife.*

One always knew where one stood with Mama, even when one longed for a bit of ambiguity.

"Women are not preserves, young Cargill." Offenbach slid a gold cravat pin through the lace at his throat. "They are wild creatures waiting for the hand of a man to tame them—for a time—then they bound away, back to the pretty parlors and comfortable boudoirs where they spin their schemes."

That characterization very likely insulted the ladies as much as referring to them as preserves did, but Offenbach spoke with such authority Charles let the matter drop.

"That is my cravat pin, Offenbach. You must have picked it up by mistake."

"Then thanks for the loan of it." Offenbach smoothed his hand over lace and linen lying just so. "I shudder to think how many more cravats I'd go through if you made me remove a perfectly placed pin and start again. Let's have a go at the maze, shall we?"

Offenbach always spoke with conviction, always laughed at his own jokes. What fascinated Charles was the degree to which this seemed to convince others that Offenbach was wise and witty.

"The maze is forbidden to guests. The gardeners told us that, and Miss Gavineau repeated the warning."

"Because she and Prescott have doubtless taken advantage of its secluded charms. We'll plead travel fatigue after supper. Always hits a day or two after arrival, when the pleasure of making landfall has paled amid the boredom that inevitably follows. While the other guests are yodeling in the music room and playing cards, or fawning over Killoway and Montmarche, we'll have a lark."

Everything with Offenbach was a lark, and most of it was aimed at either scouting out trysting locations or cozening women into investigating them. "Thank you, no. I've promised my sister I'll accompany her tonight if she sings for the other guests."

Forgive me, Phoebe. Not quite a lie, also not the stinging rebuke Offenbach deserved.

"Suit yourself, my boy. I'm off to investigate the conservatory. I saw Mrs. Cavanaugh lurking in the laburnum alley, and looking a bit lonely. Ever gallant, I will attempt to provide her the companionship she so richly deserves."

Ever randy. Offenbach was a sexual prodigy, if his own recountings were to be believed. He also knew to a vulgar degree of specificity what each lady's settlements would afford her prospective spouse.

"I'll see you at supper."

"Be that way." Offenbach bowed with a twirl of his lace-draped wrist. "You could learn a thing or two from me about how to approach the ladies, but instead you choose a priggish solitude. You'll get educated out of that eccentricity at university. The manly humors require regular activity. I don't suppose your dear mama is the lonely sort?"

Stay away from my mother. The impulse to black both of Offenbach's eyes was astonishingly fierce.

"Her ladyship prides herself on having a difficult nature. She's loyal to my father's memory and takes an exceedingly dim view of fortune hunters. Enjoy the maze, Offenbach."

"My condolences on having a dragon for a mama." Offenbach grinned and sashayed out the door.

Offenbach was repellant, with his loose talk, philandering, and trysting. He was also fascinating, as a runaway coach was fascinating. Would the passengers leap from the vehicle, risking broken bones or worse, or would they cling to the nearest handhold and pray the coachman prevailed over the fears of the horses?

Charles sought the library, which was impressive, and free of rakes and lonely women. He spared a thought for Phoebe, who should be warned of Offenbach's propensities, and for Mama.

Who was difficult, but who was not lonely, as far as Charles could tell.

～

The house party meandered onward through another three days, during which Daphne chaperoned young women trying desperately to entangle themselves with young men. She partnered Rehobeth Ingersoll at whist—ye trumpeting seraphim, *that laugh*—and watched Emma Cavanaugh advance her campaign to become the Countess of Montmarche.

Emma came down to breakfast at the same moment the earl did every morning. The implication was that they'd timed their arrivals by prearrangement, and that Montmarche sought the honor of escorting the lady to breakfast.

Mrs. Cavanaugh also lurked along the path between the stable and the house, a book in hand to excuse loitering where the earl was most likely to walk in the morning.

She involved herself with Lord Killoway, partnering him at cards, asking him to turn pages for her at the pianoforte, assuming a stepmama's privileges before becoming his step-mama in truth.

Emma was nothing if not determined, and she was young enough to provide Montmarche more children, while Daphne was old enough to recognize foolish fancies and pay them no mind. Daphne also tried to leave Charles as much to his own devices as she could, because he would turn sixteen next month, and a mama must not hover.

"Lady Cargill, good day." Absalom Offenbach made her polite bow, stepping from the forest's foliage as if a dark spell had conjured him. "Is that a gentleman's hat you have?"

They were unobserved on this quiet trail between the cemetery and the folly, which made Daphne uneasy, despite the fact that he was young enough to be her son.

"This is my own hat," she said. "It lacks ornamentation. I grew bored with the pheasant feathers. So overdone, don't you agree? One finds feathers in the forest, if one finds them anywhere."

The hat belonged to Lord Montmarche. He'd left it on the bench in the cemetery several days ago, though it appeared none the worse for having spent some time in the elements.

"Pheasant feathers are understated, and they go with almost any color save yellow. For you..." Offenbach gave her a perusal that bordered on insolent. "Dark purple feathers. A mature woman can be a trifle daring if she's looked after her figure, and your coloring would be flattered by such a hue. With a blue or green habit, trimmings a few shades lighter than aubergine would be a nice touch."

This utter drivel was offered with the sort of thoughtful expression intended to turn it into a knowledgeable opinion.

"Thank you for that suggestion. I'll wish you good day."

"No need to run off alone," he said, falling in step beside her. "I am ever willing to lend escort to a lady, regardless of differences in our age and station."

Daphne nearly pitched the earl's hat at him. He'd made that offer as if he held the higher station because she claimed the greater age.

"Aren't you concerned you'll be considered presuming, Mr. Offenbach?"

He winged his arm at her, she ignored him. "Madam, at the risk of offending, you are old enough to be my mother. In what manner could I be presuming in present company?"

What an absolute, warty, croaking toad. "A widow may choose the company she keeps, Mr. Offenbach. If you'd like my assistance gaining the favor of one of the young ladies present, you're not making a very impressive case for yourself." She stopped short of pointing out the obvious: *I am wealthy, titled, and landed in my own right. I can ruin you in a week's time.*

Antagonizing any man for no reason was foolish. Offenbach had little to lose, while Daphne had to protect both Charles and Phoebe.

"Perhaps my tastes run to an experienced variety of female."

He oozed along beside her, hands behind his back. Daphne

regretted this trip to the forest, but she'd recalled his lordship's hat, and grabbed a bonnet before she could think better of the impulse.

"If you seek to attract the notice of an older woman, then you'd best not be caught behaving like a naughty boy."

He laughed, putting Daphne in mind of Rehobeth Ingersoll.

"With the cigars, you mean? I wanted Charles to have relative privacy for his first venture into the manly art of smoking. It's easy to make a fool of oneself, and smoking indoors is frowned upon."

So drag the boy out to the garden and make a fool of him there? Daphne could think of no suitably vapid reply, so she trudged on, though the forest seemed to have grown endless.

"I must say Phoebe has a pleasant air," Offenbach mused. "She doesn't chatter, doesn't put herself forward. One appreciates that in a female."

He threatened with that compliment. Daphne grasped the threat, she didn't know what to do about it. Warn Phoebe, of course, but what if Phoebe liked Offenbach?

"The bride is the focus of all attention for this gathering," Daphne said. "The other young ladies seem to comprehend that, and to be genuinely happy for Miss Gavineau. We're walking in the direction of the fishing cottage, Mr. Offenbach. I seek to return to the house."

By myself.

"So we are," he said, though Daphne was certain he had no clue where they'd wandered. "Shall I continue walking with you, Lady Cargill?" He smiled down at her. "I can be very delicate you see, quite the proper fellow, if that's what pleases the lady."

"No need to accompany me. This track to the left leads to the stable yard, and the gardens are a short trek from there. Enjoy your rambles."

She curtseyed and moved away before Offenbach aimed any more smiles, insults, or innuendos at her. He could trouble Charles, and he could compromise Phoebe, which meant that he could create both difficulties and heartache for Daphne.

When she glanced over her shoulder, Mr. Offenbach was still standing where the paths intersected, his expression pensive. She sped up, and didn't slacken her pace until the stables came into the view. The earl was climbing down from his great black beast, and the sight of him—dusty boots, hair windblown—was unaccountably reassuring.

CHAPTER FIVE

The wedding party was one-third over.

In his mind, Lysander had made a calendar with fifteen boxes, and the top row of five boxes bore heavy black X's. Two more rows to go, and then.... What? The house would return to the blessed quiet he so treasured. Another governess had to be found, for the Dagmire creature had decamped in the middle of the night, leaving Sophronia to Henderson's long-suffering care.

The harvest looked to be decent this year, the new foals were all healthy. All was proceeding according to the annual plan, though one fewer niece was in need of a husband.

Lysander offered Sindri a final bite of carrot and let Mercer lead the beast away.

Back to work. Back to being a gracious host, a doting uncle, a dutiful papa, a potential suitor.

That last obligation rankled, while the others were merely what an earl did at his niece's wedding party. Mrs. Cavanaugh was very likely planted on the walkway near the maze, a vantage point where she could see Lysander coming from the direction of the stables or the garden.

He strode into the home wood, taking the path that bordered the stable yard.

"My lord, good day."

Lady Cargill occupied the middle of the path, though she was wearing a green dress with a brown shawl, and blended into the foliage like some sort of wood nymph, though wood nymphs did not carry top hats.

"My lady. Has the scavenger hunt ensued already?" He could think of no other reason for a woman to be carrying a top hat. "If so, I believe we're to remain with our teams, lest all of civilization be sundered by unsociability."

"The scavenger hunt is Monday," she said. "This is your hat. You left it in the cemetery and I remembered it only this morning."

He had at least a half dozen top hats with various heights of crown and curls of brims. "That is one of my favorites. I hadn't realized I'd misplaced it."

They were blocking each other's progress, and yet, Lysander would be damned if he'd ruin the glow of a hard ride by traversing the laburnum gauntlet.

"Mr. Offenbach is lurking in the forest this morning," her ladyship said. "I told him this was my hat and that I was on my way back to the house."

"Our paths take us to the same destination," Lysander said. "Does the hat fit? I have others, and I would not want Mr. Offenbach's curiosity to be aroused."

Unfortunate word choice.

The lady plopped the hat onto her head, where by virtue of abundant russet hair wound into a braided coronet, the hat did perch most fetchingly. Her temples had gone blond, in the manner of older redheads, and the hat added dash to an otherwise dignified countenance.

"A slight angle," Lysander said, adjusting the hat to the left. "There. If it was not your hat when you found it, it's your hat now." *Lucky hat.* "Was Mr. Offenbach offering you a flirtation?"

What the rutting young hound got up to was none of Lysander's business, unless Offenbach began bothering the maids.

Lady Cargill moved off up the path. "My lord, I know not what he offered, but he fills me with the same sense of foreboding I felt when the uncles presented me with Charles's first math tutor. He was all deference and manners when I was in the room. When my back was turned, he was berating my son needlessly for his own pleasure. I daresay he more than threatened to use the birch rod."

A corner of Lysander's guilty paternal conscience eased, to know other parents had been taken in by a façade of competence. His longer legs kept up with her ladyship's stride easily, though she was covering ground at a good clip.

"How did you learn of the tutor's temper?"

"I dropped into the schoolroom one warm afternoon thinking to whisk Charles to Gunter's for an ice. The wretch was whaling away so hard he didn't hear the door open. Charles's infraction was not answering quickly enough to a problem he'd not been taught how to solve."

And this small, no-longer-young woman was still furious over the hurt done to her son. She was supposed to be the inspiration for Lysander to choose a more biddable and *beddable* bride. Her example, un-dewy, un-charming, un-fertile in all likelihood, was to turn his eye in the direction of the Mrs. Cavanaughs, or—Cassandra could implement more than one strategy at once—one of Helena's girlish friends.

Instead, she reminded him that dropping into the nursery should be on his schedule.

The undeniable, inconvenient truth was that he was attracted to Lady Cargill. Physically attracted, which was more of a surprise as it related to his own urges, than it was regarding her.

He'd parted with his last mistress five years ago, and attributed a waning of interest to aging.

Perhaps his urges hadn't faded, so much as they'd at long last acquired a scintilla of common sense. Lady Cargill was attractive not only as a lover—she would be articulate and demanding in bed— but also as an ally, a source of additional resources and wisdom, a compatriot on life's forced marches.

"Charles seems to be maturing into a fine young man," Lysander said. "He sits a horse well, he is polite to the young ladies. He plays a prudent hand of whist, and he doesn't make stupid jokes."

He wasn't a junior version of Offenbach, in other words.

"My only begotten son is trying to learn how to smoke."

"You say that as if Lucifer's minions alone acquire the skill. A young man typically attempts to learn how to smoke before matriculating. Making creative wagers is another course of independent study, as is tying a cravat just so, and pissing among the fellows without appearing to inspect another man's equipment. Then there's the whole business of acting like you are heir to Casanova's legacy before you've even perfected the art of bowing over a lady's hand without seeming a fool. A young man intent on success must also present himself as a connoisseur of all sources of inebriation, while having only the most manly of tender sentiments. University life is not for the faint of heart."

Lysander had used the verb "to piss" in the presence of a lady, and that lady was amused. Her laugh was genuine and warmhearted. She laughed *with* Lysander, not at anybody's expense.

"And for the women making their debuts," her ladyship said, "there's the business of inspecting the falls of every man's breeches, admiring his thighs, and enjoying the waltz with him, all without appearing to know where babies come from."

"I thought young ladies learned of those mysteries on their wedding nights, when their husbands enlightened them." What an extraordinary conversation, and what a pleasure to speak so freely. Maria had certainly been knowledgeable on her wedding night, and what a relief that had been.

"I suppose some ladies do come to the marriage bed in ignorance, which must be quite a rude start to the marital festivities. Phoebe knows what's what, and I certainly did too."

Lady Cargill knew what was what, while Lysander was feeling a bit at sea and liking that feeling too much. "Are you concerned Mr. Offenbach will make advances toward your Phoebe?"

"Yes, and toward Charles, possibly even toward my ancient and ungracious self."

In another twelve yards, they'd break from the trees and emerge into the flowerbeds flanking the conservatory. Lysander stopped while they yet had the privacy of the woods.

"Are you tempted?"

"*Tempted?*"

"To…" He waved a hand. "Frolic. There's apparently a great deal of frolicking already in progress at Marche Hall, and Mr. Offenbach is instigating much of it. One doesn't judge, of course, but one needs to know whether to thrash the fellow or hold one's peace. He'll be gone by dawn if he's given you offense."

"You'd thrash him? For offending me?"

That hat was a distraction, a sober counterpoint to intelligent green eyes and… freckles. Lysander was noticing freckles, and next he'd be counting them, or kissing them, may God help him.

Except that this was Lady Cargill, so he'd *ask* if he might kiss her freckles before presuming to enjoy that intimacy, and the moment of asking would make him feel something precious, awkward, and difficult.

"If Offenbach requires a lesson in manners," Lysander said, "I would doubtless emerge from the encounter barely able to walk, and take to my bed for the next week. Young Offenbach would be in worse shape than I, though. I guarantee you that. Has he offended you?"

Please say yes. Offenbach wasn't even being discreet, wasn't limiting himself to an affair with one woman for the duration of the gathering.

"He does not tempt me," Lady Cargill said. "If he truly offends me, I will make it a point to tell you, for he could use a thrashing, but he's Lord Cargill's roommate. I create awkwardness there at peril to my son's regard for me."

Does anybody tempt you? Lysander would not ask that, not even in the privacy of the wood, because Lady Cargill's answer would be mercilessly honest.

"Then I will keep my figurative powder dry," Lysander said, "for now. If he brings scandal upon my house, no corner of England will be safe for him, though. Perhaps I'll remind him of that."

Lady Cargill stepped closer and removed the pin from Lysander's cravat. "Remind him with your fists, my lord?"

"With my consequence first. Surely you're aware of my impressive and far-reaching consequence?"

Those words had come out all wrong—or had they? Lady Cargill smiled as she untied his cravat, crossed the ends so what had been under was over, and retied his neckcloth into a sober and exactly symmetric mathematical.

"A streak of horse slobber was showing," she said, repositioning the pin. "Now you and your vast consequence will make a more gentlemanly impact on all who behold you."

May I kiss you? He wanted to ask that question, wanted to gift her with all the respect and interest it embodied. He also truly longed to kiss her, not merely to wander the woods with her while putting off his duties as a host.

Ten more days until sanity returned—unless he proposed to Emma Cavanaugh, in which case, more foolishness would ensue for a time.

"Shall we continue on to the house?" Lysander asked.

Lady Cargill looked him over, her gaze critical, as if assessing a portrait in progress. She ran her fingers through his hair several times, bringing him the scent of orange blossoms.

"That's better," she said, starting toward the break in the trees. "Are you sure you wouldn't like your hat back?"

He'd like his heart back, for the damned woman appeared to be making off with it, which was perishing inconvenient of her.

"You may keep the hat, though you must promise me that should I allow two waltzes at the wedding ball, you will save one of them for me."

Out into the sunlight she marched, Lysander trailing like a sleeper reluctant to face the dawn.

"Of course, my lord. It would be an honor to dance with you. Thank you for your escort,

He bowed, though she'd already moved away in the direction of the house. Had a fine walk, did Lady Cargill. And a fine sense of humor.

And freckles.

∞

"Lady Cargill cannot be compromised," Offenbach said. "I've had more than a week to consider the notion and it can't be done."

Mr. Terrence Cargill sniffed at his ale and set the tankard down untasted. "Because you ain't got the stomach for it? You needn't bed the fair Daphne. All you have to do is create the fiction that she's been free with her favors."

Offenbach had no illusions about himself. He was randy, profligate, ornamental at best, and not very nice. He yet had standards, tarnished though they were, and Terrence Cargill offended those standards.

"Lady Cargill might be mature, but she is attractive nonetheless." She had that indefinable quality of spirit, of directed energy, which intrigued a fellow whose greatest purpose in life was to avoid paying for anything. "Her ladyship's age is not the problem." Besides, Offenbach had learned years ago that Mr. Heyward's aphorism was correct: *When all candles be out, all cats be grey.*

For this interview, Mr. Cargill had appropriated the private dining room at the Duck and Donkey, a humble coaching inn eight miles from the splendors of Marche Hall. The summer ale was superb, and the tavern maids comely and friendly.

"If her age ain't putting you off," Cargill said, sitting back, "then be about the business. I ain't paying you to learn the secrets of Montmarche's famed maze." Cargill was perhaps ten years Offenbach's senior, and he carried at least two stone more evidence of prosperity about his middle. He gave orders as if he, not his nephew, had inherited the title.

"What puts me off, Cargill, is the lady herself. Nobody will believe she's granted me her favors. She's not that sort of widow. She took one look at me and knew me for a bounder." Worse, she'd communicated that judgment clearly, not bothering with the usual house party polite fictions.

Her ladyship had regarded Offenbach as if he were dung on her slipper. He should be furious with her for presuming to judge him, except he *was* dung on her slipper. Dung whose creditors were ready to toss him into the sponging house, where all of society's impecunious excreta collected like a crossing sweeper's pile of horse droppings, but not half so useful.

"Then convince her ladyship you're worth another look," Cargill said, rising. "She's a little bit of a thing. Wrestle her into a linen closet, lame her horse and take advantage on the long walk back to the stables. She wanders the countryside with her easel. Come upon her within view of some walking party and claim passion outstripped your good sense."

"You are prodigiously talented at planning a woman's ruin, but how do I manage the little business of being charged with rape?"

"If she accuses you of rape, she'll be lying, won't she? You've said as much. Mutton dressed up as lamb and all that."

Offenbach felt a moment's sympathy for young Lord Cargill. Terrence was the boy's oldest male relation, and a venal, greedy, disgrace despite being born to significant privilege.

"Why can't I ruin Phoebe? She's a spinster in the making and needs a spot of adventure." She did not need all the wealth that was rumored to languish amid her settlement accounts. She bore the restless air of a woman overdue for a few rash kisses.

"If you ruin my niece, you'd have to marry her. Damned Daphne would tie up the settlements so neither you nor I would see a groat. Ruin Daphne and even her perishing brother will agree that her opinions ain't to be trusted, and then I'll finally get control of his lordship's fortune. Failing all else, you might be able to get to the boy."

"Another criminal act." And the boy would be horrified at the very notion. That Offenbach was only mildly revolted at such a venal scheme was lowering indeed.

Cargill looked unconvinced. "You needn't climb into his bed to inspire a case of hero worship. Goad him into insisting that Daphne turn loose of his funds. My guiding but generous hand would be the logical check on his youthful impulses."

Cargill would part with his nephew's coin about as willingly as Mephistopheles would return a damned soul to the custody of the seraphim.

"Lord Cargill won't become infatuated with me in the next eight days, not to the extent that he'd cast aspersion on his mother's handling of his funds. He respects his mother and will never stand for her to be criticized before others."

Which was... touching, if a bit silly. Lady Cargill was merely a woman with some means, not a goddess of maternal perfection. She was fierce though, unlike her children.

"Then," Terrence said, "you are back to compromising the mother. Daphne has been a thorn in my side since my brother took a notion to marry a squire's daughter. She can keep her settlements, she can keep her daughter's settlements, but for the boy's money to be in her hands is unnatural. You either give me the means to induce her to sign that money over to me, or you will wish you had. Good day, Mr. Offenbach."

Not so fast. "Pay the shot," Offenbach said, not bothering to get to his feet.

"I *beg* your pardon?"

Offenbach took a sip of the ale. "Pay for the bloody bread and ale. If you want me to ruin a woman who has done me no wrong, betray the trust of a mere boy, and risk the wrath of an earl who is reported to be a damned fine hand with a firearm, then you can absorb the cost of a pitcher of ale."

Of the three wrongs... Offenbach could not choose among them. Betraying a boy's trust was very low. Compromising a decent woman was vile. Courting Montmarche's ire was stupid beyond belief, for the earl was the old-fashioned sort, who would take any slight to a guest as a slight to his own honor.

The older generation took quaint notions like honor seriously, bless them.

Still Cargill merely stood by the door, looking well fed and late for an appointment with his tailor.

"I will tell the fair Daphne all," Offenbach said, "if you think to use me ill. You will never see a penny of that money, and I will be a hero."

Cargill laughed. "Oh, right. Force yourself upon my sister-in-law, drag her into the maze with malice aforethought, aid my plans as long as they aid yours, then turn your back on me. See how worshipfully polite society regards you then, Offenbach. You were born a scoundrel, the least you can do is be competent about it. Daphne will hand that money over to me before she brings ruin down on the heads of her children. You merely have to bring scandal down on *her*."

Cargill tossed a coin onto the table and strode out.

Two nights ago, Offenbach had taken a large ball of twine and explored the maze. He'd been nowhere near the center when the twine had run out, and he'd wasted more than an hour making wrong turns, doubling back, and making more wrong turns.

Cargill's challenge was like the maze: All wrong turns, no way to reach the treasure. Except...

Offenbach sipped his ale, for not a drop should be wasted, and flirted with the tavern maids. He munched on fresh bread with fresh butter, and considered the problem of compromising Lady Cargill.

He also considered the pleasures of the sponging house. Beatings weren't the worst of it, and the usual progression was from sponging house to debtor's prison, a quagmire that never released its victims save in a shroud or longing for one.

As Offenbach peered into the bottom of his tankard, a glimmer of an idea germinated in his weary and worried mind.

Lady Cargill must be compromised, that was given and something he was well equipped to accomplish. Offenbach merely needed to be *found* embracing her, or sharing a linen closet with her. A gentlemanly silence on his part paired with protestations of innocence from her would ignite a bonfire of gossip, and the lady's ruin would result.

What was needed was an ally, somebody who could be depended upon to discover a couple at an unfortunate moment, and trumpet that news all over Marche Hall. The damage would be done, and—such a pity—Offenbach would be victimized by circumstances every bit as much as the lady. He'd nobly offer marriage, she'd turn him down flat, and all would be well.

Perfect.

○

"Perhaps your lordship could help me find a book?" Mrs. Cavanaugh had developed an affliction of the eyelids, for she seemed compelled to bat them at Lysander like one plagued by a nervous tic.

He'd sought the quiet of the library at mid-afternoon, while his guests rested from the day's archery contest. Nobody had been shot in the arse, though Phoebe had demonstrated an accuracy that had the young men regarding her more closely—and more respectfully.

Lady Cargill, alas, had declined to take up a weapon, while her son had also shown himself to good advantage. Without being told as much, Lysander knew that the mother's skill eclipsed that of her children, though she would leave all the accolades to them.

"What sort of reading do you favor?" Lysander asked Mrs. Cavanaugh. He did not glance past her shoulder to ensure the door was open, for that would be the behavior of a rude or worried man.

Mrs. Cavanaugh was a pleasant woman with enough experience of life and marriage to partner Lysander in a cordial, fruitful union.

He should use this moment to further investigate the possibility.

"I favor deferring to the judgment of the man who owns the library," Mrs. Cavanaugh said. "Of all the treasures here, which do you suggest I sample in the limited time remaining to me at Marche Hall?"

Subtle, that was not. The look she sent Lysander was probably intended to excite his manly humors. She was a handsome woman, a robust blond who would age well, and yet...

She had four boys, whom Lysander would be expected to stepparent. Four of the little darlings, all male, poised like penguins before a pool, to dive one by one into the perils of adolescence. She had not one but two sets of former in-laws, and if anybody liked to meddle with a man's peace, it was relatives of the distant in-law variety.

"You seem to enjoy novels," Lysander said. "Have you read all of Sir Walter's offerings? He and Mrs. Radcliffe are side by side on the shelves beneath Lord Killoway's portrait.

The painting had been done as George had left behind the first trapping of boyhood. His facial bones were emerging from the roundness of childhood, his gaze was becoming not merely curious but educated. This version of George seemed to regard his father exactly as Lysander had regarded his son at that age:

Steady on, my boy. Perils ahead, keep a sharp eye and cool head. Though what did a man on the brink of his sixth decade have in common with a young fellow going off to public school?

"I do favor an entertaining tale," Mrs. Cavanaugh said. "This is a fine portrait. I should have one done of my boys, though I can't imagine all four of them holding still long enough to sit to anybody."

"Have it done now," Lysander said. "For soon they will be scattered to the winds of time and fate, and such a portrait will mean a great deal to them and to their progeny."

She approached George's portrait, peering at the signature. "My lord, may I speak honestly?"

Must you? "Of course."

"I do not enjoy the widowed state. Many women tout its freedoms, but I suspect they do so out of a need to appear content with a situation they are powerless to change. If blunt speaking will alter my circumstances for the better, then I will risk appearing forward and speak up."

The dratted woman had closed the door. Lysander planted himself by the window with the best view of the gardens, a gamble. If she plastered herself to his person where anybody in the garden could see, he was compromised, but would she be so bold?

"I am known to be direct myself," Lysander said, lacing his hands behind his back. "Do go on."

"You have only the one heir, my lord. I've studied DeBrett's and had occasion to hear your sister lamenting the lack of spares. She worries exceedingly as I know your nieces do as well. Should anything happen to you and Lord Killoway, the earldom would revert to the crown."

And reversion to the crown, as every peer's son knew, was a failure of duty so monstrous as to exceed mortal sins and hanging felonies.

"You are admonishing me to take another wife," Lysander said. "My dear sister has done the same."

Mrs. Cavanaugh's smile was that of a governess whose charge had recited the entire royal succession without a blunder.

"You take my point. I knew you were a man of insight. I've written as much to my sons."

All four of them, no doubt. The male sons of the masculine gender. Those sons, though at least two of them were likely too young to read.

"My sister does share your concern, though you will be pleased to know that most of the Marche wealth is personal rather than entangled with the title."

Her brows rose, as much consternation as a lady on campaign could show, though the point was valid. None of the Marches would end up destitute if the succession failed. Not nearly.

"I'm pleased for the sake of your family to hear that, my lord, but what of Marche Hall? Shall you go to your reward knowing that our sovereign, ever one to squander wealth, sold this magnificent property to fund another dome on his Pavilion?"

She was arguing sense to him as she crossed the library, and yet, her version of sense did not appeal to Lysander half so much as Daphne Cargill's did.

"I have distant cousins," Lysander said, "in America. My father corresponded with them, and I had a letter a year or two ago. I'm planning on writing back." Had just that moment made the decision to pen those cousins a friendly note. Really should have done it two years ago.

"Americans?" She wrinkled her nose. "I suppose that's better than nothing, but who's to say how an American will treat your nieces and sisters should they become dependent upon him in their old age?"

This was not a courtship or even a flirtation, this was a lecture, one Lysander had heard from his sister and his own conscience often enough. Had Lady Cargill shown any interest in Lysander as a man, had she complained of the burdens of the widowed state, he might well be...

But she hadn't. Just the opposite.

"Mrs. Cavanaugh, I do appreciate your concern for my family, and I will consider your words. For me to remarry a suitable partner would be nothing more than common sense, and in all likelihood, the kindest gesture I could make toward my son and family. I am considering remarriage very seriously, though I'll thank you to keep that admission in confidence."

Her countenance changed, from guarded graciousness to joy, and something else. In her eyes, Lysander caught a flash of desperate relief.

The poor woman did not simply long to remarry, she needed to. Creditors, perhaps, or unkind family that did not treat her sons well. Perhaps she had gambling debts to settle, or had acquired followers whose lack of discretion was poised to sully her good name.

She longed to remarry for the institution itself, not for the man who'd share it with her.

"I knew you for a sensible, dutiful man the first time we danced, my lord. Your conversation was intelligent without being boring, your partnering on the dancefloor competent without calling attention to itself. I knew you were worthy of my esteem, and my judgment has been vindicated."

She gazed up at him, as if willing him to offer a reciprocal compliment. A betrothal started in such a moment with such a glance. He should admit to esteeming her similarly—for her poise, charm, or some other similarly insubstantial quality—she'd smile knowingly. They'd exchange more innuendos and glances, *and an understanding would be born.*

Lysander longed to open the window and bellow for his horse.

"I should hope," he said, "that a decent education and my dancing master's tireless efforts were for some worthy purpose. We never did find you a book."

Again, her eyes gave her away. Her smile remained fixed, but her gaze faltered from hopeful to determined. Lysander saw the moment she decided to kiss him, saw that strategy graduate from a potential choice to a battlefield option to a necessary maneuver.

Turn from her, walk away. Even duty should be chosen on a man's own terms.

Mrs. Cavanaugh leaned closer, her eyelids lowered. "My lord, I must impose more honesty on you."

Climb out the damned window. Cough. Be assailed by a blinding megrim. And yet, Lysander stood there, feeling sorry for Mrs. Cavanaugh, and knowing what his duty was.

"Perhaps not," he said. "Perhaps your admission need not be made."

Another peeping glance, and Lysander's heart ached. Maria would not want to see him married to a woman who spoke vows in desperation. Maria would understand why four step-sons was a daunting prospect. Maria would know what to say to diffuse the entire situation without offending anybody.

And Maria was gone.

"I yet grieve," Lysander said.

"We all do," Mrs. Cavanaugh retorted, closing the last of the distance between them. "For our youth, for our happy memories, for our wasted powers. We grieve but duty yet calls to us, if we are honorable."

Another lecture, delivered from very close range. From kissing range.

Maria, help me. But Maria could not. Duty was duty, and Mrs. Cavanaugh was a willing partner in that duty.

She closed her eyes, put a hand on Lysander's chest, and was half-way up on her toes when the door opened.

"Good afternoon, my lord, ma'am." Young Lord Cargill had a book in his hand. "I thought to return borrowed treasure and perhaps find another tome. Why is it that at school, one always has one's nose in a book, but one never seems to truly read?"

The lad sent an admiring glance around to the library's myriad shelves. He wandered into the room, and—blessings upon his house unto the nineteenth generation—he left the damned door wide open.

"Ivanhoe belongs over here," he said, "as best I recall. Is that a portrait of Lord Killoway? He bears a resemblance to you, sir, about the eyes and mouth. Perhaps you'd like to have a go at Ivanhoe, Mrs. Cavanaugh?"

Yes, please, have a go at Ivanhoe.

The moment Lord Cargill had stepped into the room, Mrs. Cavanaugh had stepped back as if Lysander's coat had burst into flames.

"I believe I've already read that one," she said. "That's the story with the knights and intrigues and castles and whatnot, isn't it?"

Lord Cargill studied the book in his hand, and Lysander knew exactly what the boy was thinking: *What does a gentleman say to that?*

"The very one," Lysander replied. "Much traveling about, lurking in forests, and longing for what cannot be."

Mrs. Cavanaugh moved toward the door. "Not a very happy tale. I'll leave you gentlemen to your literature. My lord, pleasant chatting with you, as always. I do hope you can resolve your difficulties in the very near future."

And my bedroom door will be unlocked all the while.

Though perhaps not. A woman who'd borne four children might insist on waiting until the wedding night, though she'd also likely insist on a short engagement.

Lysander took Lord Cargill by the arm and turned him toward the door. "Thank you, my boy. I don't know if you meant to intrude, but your interruption was so timely, I'm tempted to remember you in my will."

"She stalks you," he said quietly. "Offenbach pointed it out, envying you the lady's attentions, I think. Phoebe mentioned it as well in discussions with Miss Gavineau when they thought I was absorbed in my reading. When I asked Mama if Mrs. Cavanaugh was pursuing you, Mama grew quiet and changed the subject. Mama is never one to keep an opinion to herself."

Lysander walked with Cargill down the corridor and opened the door to the estate office, a room guests were not permitted access to.

"You discussed my situation with your mother?" He crossed to the decanters and poured a drink. "Join me in a tot?"

"Before dinner, sir?"

"After an ambush. I stock only good quality spirits, young man. Not that swill Offenbach likely has in his flask."

His lordship grinned, looking very much like his mother. "I would be remiss to pass up an opportunity to drink good brandy in good company. I haven't discussed you with my mother, though. She dodged the topic both times I brought it up, which is unlike her."

Lysander poured the lad a short serving. Good spirits or not, he was a slender fellow with some growing yet to do. He had doubtless yet to acquire much of a head for liquor.

"Your mother is wonderfully forthright," Lysander said. "If she dodged the topic, it's likely because my social calendar didn't interest her. To her health."

Cargill drank to that, and even appeared to appreciate his brandy. "Perhaps Mama has no interest in who is keeping you company, sir, but why do you suppose my mama, a woman of much resolve and clarity of purpose, was crying when last I passed her door?"

CHAPTER SIX

"Are you upset because I've once again failed to attach anybody's interest?" Phoebe asked.

Her question bore none of the inchoate drama Daphne would have expected. "Of course not," Daphne said, drawing the brush through her unbound hair. "Do you expect to have a man swooning at your feet on less than two weeks' notice?"

Please do not tell me Offenbach has caught your eye. Daphne had seen him watching Phoebe, but then, he watched all the ladies, all the servants, and even the other young men.

"Men don't swoon," Phoebe said, taking the brush from Daphne's hand. "I've wondered if that's why they drink to excess, because they are not permitted to swoon."

Years ago, Daphne had brushed her daughter's hair every night, though that was a maid's task. The ritual had soothed both mother and daughter at the end of the day, and given them time to simply talk.

When had Daphne let the gift of simply talking with her daughter slip through her fingers?

"You might well be right," she said. "A lady can faint, and all cares and worries fade for a time as others tend to her welfare. Men have no comparable means of escape, though nobody will whisper that they are increasing merely because their corsets were laced too tightly."

In the vanity mirror's reflection, Phoebe smiled. "You are an original, Mama. I will never be like you, which I suspect is a great relief to our menfolk."

The brush continued to work its magic, and some of Daphne's upset eased to mere annoyance. "I am dratted sick and tired of ordering my life to please our menfolk, and I'm too old to be an original." Every year, the wheat blond gained ground over the red in her hair, which Daphne liked. The effect was dramatic, and not something any hairdresser could create with powder and dye. Witches, crones, and oracles had hair like Daphne's. "Perhaps I am an eccentric."

Phoebe set the brush aside and divided Daphne's hair into two skeins, then further divided the right skein into three.

"You had a letter from Uncle Terrence, didn't you, Mama?"

"You peeked?"

"I know his signature. He sent me enough sermons and warning when I was off at school. Half the time he was praising Cousin Jasper's many fine qualities, the other half he was warning me not to turn into a hoyden, lest fine young men like Jasper disdain my company."

She braided deftly, which made it difficult for Daphne to turn. "You never told me this."

"You had enough to worry about, and letters are only letters. I knew Jasper would never be more than his father's toady, and that Uncle sought to keep my wealth in the Cargill family. Papa warned me about that."

And a warning from a quiet, soft-spoken papa was an admonition worth heeding.

"Thank you for recalling the warning. Jasper as a son-in-law would give me the collywobbles."

Phoebe finished the first braid and tied it off with a red ribbon. "Did Uncle's letter upset you?"

"Yes."

Phoebe began on the second braid. "And? Have you been caught stargazing from the center of the maze with Mr. Offenbach? Smoking cigars in the conservatory? Tippling at breakfast?"

"Uncle Terrence laments that he allowed me to bring Charles with us. Terrence has heard tales of drunkenness regarding young Lord Cargill. He claims gossip has reached him that Charles stinks of cheap cigars and cheaper liquor, and is learning to flirt with widows twice his age."

"Somebody's lying," Phoebe said. "Lord Montmarche would never permit drunkenness or overtly lewd behavior from a guest. He'd take Charles aside and deliver a quiet, terrifying scold or two, and Charles would mend his ways—except Charles has no ways to mend."

This loyalty between siblings was one of Daphne's greatest joys. "Uncle Terrence has a gifted imagination. Why do you think I've been so disinclined to flirt or dally myself? Terrence is waiting to pounce, to announce my licentious nature, my disregard for propriety, my bad judgment. I drink wine only modestly, I dance only with happy husbands and balding bachelors."

Phoebe tied off the second braid. "I'm sorry Mama. I see the other ladies here—Mrs. Ingersoll, for example—and I realize that my mother is not who Uncle Terrence would have me believe she is."

"Oh?"

"Those letters from Uncle Terrence did not exactly sing your praises. At family gatherings, Uncle approaches me as if I'm to be pitied because I am your daughter. Charles pointed that out, and he's right, even if he is my little brother."

"You and Charles have been talking, haven't you?"

Phoebe hugged Daphne around the shoulders, an extraordinary display about which a mother dare not remark.

"How is it possible I've missed my brother? And yet, I have." She took the dressing stool at the side of the vanity. "He's been off to public school, I've been in Town socializing, but someone has taken the naughty boy he was and replaced him with a young gentleman who's taller than me. Public school hasn't ruined him. I hope university doesn't either."

"My sentiments exactly. Has anybody here caught your eye, Phoebe?"

"Yes, in a manner of speaking."

Daphne waited, because Phoebe had never ventured an interest in any particular gentleman. She'd been too busy trying to get the young fools to notice her.

"Helena has caught my interest."

A beat of silence went by, while Daphne kept her features neutral and mentally rehearsed the I-will-love-you-forever-no-matter-what speech, though Phoebe's admission was rather a surprise.

"Helena and Mr. Prescott," Phoebe went on. "They aren't madly in love, or they don't appear to be. She is *five-and-twenty*, Mama, and he is nearly thirty. They aren't in each other's pockets, they aren't perpetually emerging from alcoves looking mussed and pleased. They don't insist on partnering each other at everything from whist to waltzing."

Daphne put away her speech—for now. "But you sense they will be happy together."

"Not merely happy. They are already a couple in a manner you and Papa were. They communicate without words, they are connected by more than physical attraction. They like and respect one another and are undertaking their vows as *vows*, not as... I don't know, a social display."

I am so proud of you. That speech too, would have to wait for another time, lest the moment be ruined by Phoebe's natural self-consciousness.

Or Daphne's. "Love comes in many forms," she said, "and it changes. Your father and I started out with a good deal of physical attraction, but I also enjoyed his company and respected him. He was like young Lord Killoway in that—quiet, attentive rather than arrogant. His sense of humor rescued us from argument many times, as did his ability to hold his tongue until I had settled enough to be reasoned with."

"You?" Phoebe's brows drew down. "Needing to settle? The mind boggles." She rose and stretched like the lithe young creature she was. "My staid and proper mama, needing to settle. How absurd the notion."

Phoebe hugged Daphne again and moved toward the door. "Will you be relieved to go home, Mama? I shall be. This gathering has been enjoyable, and Marche Hall is a lovely property, but two weeks is long enough. Charles agrees with me on that."

Daphne regarded the woman in the mirror. Braids made her look like some kind of Valkyrie, particularly with the red bows, and the streaking at her temples.

"Charles was eager to join us at this house party. Now you tell me he's eager to return home?"

"Mr. Offenbach tried to teach him to smoke cigars, and Charles obliged him the once, but doesn't care to make another attempt. I suspect Charles is leaving much out of the telling, but his roommate's company has failed to enchant him."

"Cigars, brandy, and dalliance appear to fill Mr. Offenbach's entire calendar—and sleeping off excesses of same. I'll see you at supper."

"We're to have another buffet tonight. Mr. Tremont has asked me to sit with him." And Phoebe was, however subtly, asking for her mother's opinion on a matter of some import.

"Mr. Tremont doesn't take himself too seriously," Daphne said. "I like that in a man. He'll be good company." He was also a viscount's spare, nearly thirty, and had a shipping business with a maternal uncle.

"I do too," Phoebe said. "He isn't silly or vain."

"Ask if he's attending the Wyand's party in September. A man willing to make up numbers is always welcome, and I'm thinking of accepting Lady Wyand's invitation."

Phoebe's smile was prettier than she could possibly know. "I'll ask him."

She slipped out the door, and Daphne again felt the pull of tears, though not because Terrence was at his usual carping and lying.

"My babies are growing up, not simply growing older," Daphne informed her reflection. And Phoebe and Charles were turning out to be fine human beings. "I have children to be proud of. Even Terrence cannot refute that reality."

Though, being Terrence, he would try.

∽

"Sir, might I ask you a question?" Young Lord Cargill studied his drink, but he didn't blush. For a lad of fifteen, he was self-possessed, and he knew not to guzzle fine spirits.

"You may."

"Just how *does* one go on with the ladies?" The boy held his drink up to the sunbeams pouring through the estate office window. "Not that I'll be doing any *going on* with them just yet. Perhaps I mean how does one go on with the ladies who aren't strictly ladies, though they are ever so friendly and pretty. One hears tales of what transpires at university..."

And *one*, being a perceptive lad, had seen what went on at even a tame house party.

"It's a mystery, isn't it?" Lysander replied. "How to be a gentleman and a man, particularly a young man in certain areas of life?" He'd had this discussion with his own father, and with George, more than once. He'd heard grandfathers musing on the same topic at the clubs, though their rendition usually began with: *In my day....*

"Offenbach makes it sound so easy," Cargill replied. "First, you scout out all the possible trysting locations that are both convenient, reasonably comfortable, and private. Then, when others are unlikely to observe, you look the lady in the eye with naughtiness on your mind. Next, you drop a few verbal hints, referring to nature or art. You brush up against the woman as if by accident. She brushes up against you or stumbles into your embrace. She returns your bold looks with flirtatious glances. And then,"—he waved a slim hand—"heigh ho, and off to the hermit's grotto."

Offenbach had a list, like steps to a dance. How crass. "That's one approach, but what is it an approach to?"

"Every hour of the day and evening, to hear Offenbach tell it."

Lady Cargill had been right about Offenbach, too right, apparently. "And does Offenbach strike you as happy? As a man to emulate?"

Cargill propped a hip on the window ledge, looking both elegant and boyish. "He's pathetic, if I may speak honestly in confidence. I'd rather not follow his example, but the ladies allow him certain privileges."

"Some ladies, for which we do not judge them." Lysander took the reading chair near the second window. "When it comes to intimate matters, they are all ladies and we must comport ourselves as gentlemen, whether we keep them company for an hour or a lifetime. What varies is how much of our affection they seek and on what terms."

Cargill was listening, for all he appeared to be fascinated with the garden below.

"You let the lady know what your terms are," Lysander said, "she lets you know what her terms are. There's either agreement or not, and you wish each other well at the conclusion of the negotiation, regardless of its outcome. You pay attention, *you ask*, you offer the woman honesty. You *never* assume and take liberties because that's a good way to give offense or end up facing a pistol on the field of foolishness."

That earned him a signature Cargill smile. Lysander was coming to know the look. "Never heard it called that before."

"Blowing out a chap's brains because he spoke unfortunately is perhaps the only thing worse than having your own brains splattered for the same stupid reason. Honest discourse with women takes courage, and you won't always express yourself well. Experience improves your ability to discern when witty banter is sought, and when a bold proposition is in order. I daresay focusing on the witty banter for now will stand you in good stead. Too many fellows seek only to perfect their bold propositions, and some ladies take us all into dislike as result."

Cargill finished his drink. "Witty banter, sir?"

"I haven't any. Watch Tremont. The man's a favorite with the ladies because he's funny, smart, and never vulgar. Prescott comports himself similarly, and then there's Offenbach, who, if we are to be frank, was added to the guest list to serve as a bad example. Makes a complete ass of himself but keeps the merry widows and bored wives from plaguing the likes of you and me."

"While he steals my jewelry and calls it borrowing. Phoebe and Mama don't care for him."

Which, to Cargill's credit, the boy took seriously. "The ladies have had to learn to trust their instincts, Cargill. If you mis-read a fellow, he'll make a nuisance of himself over a few hands of cards. If the ladies make that mistake, it can mean their ruin. Trust the ladies, and when they give you their trust, never betray it."

"Latin is much simpler," Cargill said, leaving the window sill to set his glass on the sideboard.

"Latin has its place. Why do you suppose your mama was upset?" Lysander could have blustered on, about an upset guest being cause for a host's concern, but Cargill was a canny lad—very much his mother's son—and would see right through that.

"She received a letter from Uncle Terrence. He's greedy, arrogant, and refuses to believe that we can manage without his interference. He wants our money, and we are not inclined to give it to him. Uncle Frederick is getting on though—he's my guardian and Mama's brother—so Mama worries."

"Getting on, how?"

"He's older than Mama by a considerable patch. They have different mothers, and Uncle Frederick's heart pains him. He's stout, gouty, and loves his port, but insists he'll live until I'm one and twenty purely to thwart Uncle Terrence."

The boy worried too, apparently for good reason. "Families are the very devil, some families."

Cargill crossed to the door, his stride the loose-limbed blessing of a very young fellow. "What will you do about Mrs. Cavanaugh? Shall I keep watch for you like a chaperone?"

What a kind young man he was, and shrewd like his mama. "Does Tremont fancy her? They would be nearly of an age."

"I haven't seen any particular attraction there, sir. Mrs. Cavanaugh is well to do, according to Offenbach. She has two settlements, he says, and she need not consider Mr. Tremont simply on the basis of his situation."

Young Tremont was a favorite with the ladies, while Lysander was *getting on*. Of course Mrs. Cavanaugh had chosen the fellow for whom there was virtually no competition.

"Keep watch," Lysander said. "I'd take it as a personal favor if you'd discreetly keep watch."

Cargill winked, saluted with two fingers, and jaunted out the door.

The moaning began after midnight.

Daphne had sought the shelter of Mrs. Gavineau's company at dinner, the better to ignore Mrs. Cavanaugh's compulsion to sit nearly in Lord Montmarche's lap. Phoebe had taken supper with Mr. Tremont, and Charles had joined their party.

Which was as matters should have gone, and yet, Daphne had trouble finding sleep.

Then an odd, low, warbling moan had sounded from the far side of the bedroom wall. Not a sound of terror, but neither was it pleasant.

Daphne donned her dressing gown, pulled on a pair of wool stockings, and let herself into the corridor. The moaning came from the bedroom on the far side of Daphne's chamber, another guest room.

A door clicked open across the way, and the Montmarche stood in the shadows cast by the hall sconces.

"No more house parties," he said. "Not until I lose most of my hearing. As your host, I apologize for that racket."

"Do you suppose someone's in distress?"

The moaning crested higher and acquired a particular vibrato.

"Mrs. Ingersoll is assigned to that room," Montmarche said, taking Daphne by the wrist. "I shudder to think who is inspiring her to such raptures."

Mrs. Inger—? "Oh, I see. *Raptures*. Well then."

Montmarche led her back to his open door. "The look on your face, my lady, is priceless. You are trying not to laugh, because you know if you allow yourself any display of mirth, you'll dissolve into whoops, and the footman on the landing will come at a dead run, and then Sophronia will scamper down from the nursery, and we'll have a scandal of royal proportions."

Warbling graduated to thrilling as Montmarche pulled Daphne into a sitting room and closed the door.

He guffawed, then chuckled, and Daphne's composure went completely to pot. "Raptures have never sounded so... so...." She dissolved into renewed laughter.

"Precisely," Montmarche said. "Raptures have never sounded so. It's as if the happy couple seeks to be discovered, but we must not oblige them."

"Raptures," Daphne said, chortling heartily. "Heaven help me. I'll never be able to look a lover in the eye again, not that I expect to have any lovers." How good it felt to laugh out loud. "How does a man keep his concentration amid all that racket?"

Montmarche drew a handkerchief from the pocket of his dressing gown. "Men are amazingly focused under some circumstances, and amazingly easy to distract under others, largely for the same reasons." He passed Daphne the handkerchief. "Ah, the silence. Cupid's arrow is apparently spent for the nonce."

The moaning, warbling, and trilling had ceased, and the late night quiet was more profound for the contrast.

"I should go back to my room," Daphne said, dabbing at her eyes. "Though if Cupid's arrow takes flight again, I will not answer for the consequences."

"I'd wait a few moments," Montmarche said. "If Mrs. Ingersoll is entertaining Mr. Offenbach, he'll be sneaking down the corridor any moment now. He's not one to linger over his pleasures, apparently. Would you care for a brandy?"

Daphne offered the earl his handkerchief. "A tot to settle my nerves?"

"Keep it." He opened a low cabinet that also served as a table between two reading chairs facing the hearth. "I offer you hospitality because I enjoy your company. Then too, I'd hate for you to encounter Mr. Offenbach in an awkward moment."

"I would not mind in the least catching him out at his silly games."

Montmarche set two glasses on the table and poured a serving into each. "But then he'd have grounds to inquire as to where you'd been wandering at this late hour. Can't have that, can we?"

He passed her a glass, and touched his drink to hers. "To house parties concluded without drama."

Daphne drank to that, but why must the house party conclude with only a handful of truly enjoyable moments, all of them spent with her host?

"Shall we sit?" Daphne asked. "This Armagnac is to be savored."

Montmarche regarded her, amusement lingering in his eyes, and something more. "An excellent suggestion. I find having a house full of people whom I am expected to entertain and be endlessly gracious to taxing, and yet, at the end of the day..."

He waited for Daphne to take one of the wing chairs.

"At the end of the day," Daphne said, "you would sleep more easily if you could recount your domestic adventures with somebody who was also sharing hers?"

"Something like that."

Firelight might hide age, dust, and wrinkles, as the saying went, but it also fostered a mood of shared confidences. Daphne tucked her feet up and prepared to enjoy her host's exclusive company one last time.

"Your house party has gone well," she said. "No smoldering disagreements, no scandals, no food poisoning, nobody refusing to speak to anybody else. You and Lady Cassandra have shown your guests a wonderful time."

The earl made a handsome picture, drink in hand, the brocade dressing gown testifying to both his wealth and his inherent dignity even when informal. Daphne shoved aside the question of what he'd look like without his clothes. He'd look like a man. She'd seen her share of those.

"My sister's agenda for this gathering extended beyond providing genteel entertainment."

"She'll want to see her daughter married of course, but first we must get through tomorrow's scavenger hunt." The wedding would happen on Saturday in the family chapel, and Sunday, the final day of the gathering, would be for rest, and then Monday the guests departed.

"What were your objectives for these two weeks?" he asked. "Beyond painting the distant reaches of the park."

Daphne had spent several fine days in his lordship's deer park, and she had some excellent renditions of Marche Hall to show for it.

"I wanted Charles to gain some experience in good society, and for Phoebe to spend time with friends."

He set down his drink and took Daphne's hand. "But what do

you want *for yourself*, my lady? I know the dreaded uncle has plagued you even while you bide as my guest, and that vexes me beyond bearing. Who the hell is he to question the terms of his brother's will, when clearly, both of your children—whose rearing has been left almost exclusively in your hands—are more than decent people?"

Montmarche's grasp was warm and firm, and pleased Daphne for too many reasons.

"I suspect Terrence's debts are mounting. He has expensive tastes, and four daughters. He also knows Charles is losing the last vestiges of impressionable boyhood, and if Phoebe remains unmarried at age twenty-five, she gains access to her own funds."

Daphne fell silent rather than descend into outright babbling.

Montmarche kept hold of her hand, stroking his thumb across her knuckles. He offered not a gesture of friendship, but a lover's overture. He and Daphne were adults, he need not send her a scented invitation.

"Tell me what you want, Daphne. I know the question is difficult, because I've been considering it myself."

Daphne. Nobody called her by name, and that was at her insistence. She was Lady Cargill, the better to have some consequence when consequence was needed.

She did not need or want her consequence now. She longed to be simply Daphne, enjoying a brief, discreet moment with a man she esteemed very much. Such an opportunity might never befall her again, and as goodnight waltzes went, Montmarche would be a splendid partner.

"I want you," she said. "Right now, Montmarche, I want you."

CHAPTER SEVEN

Many more encounters with Rehobeth Ingersoll, and I will lose my wits and my hearing.

"Ready for another round?" the lady asked, stroking her hand over Offenbach's belly.

Have mercy. He'd exerted himself for the sake of a larger plan, and desperately needed the solace of his own bed.

"Alas, my dear, I am billeted with young Lord Cargill. I can tell him I was enjoying Marche Hall's library, but even he won't believe I stayed up all night with the philosophers." Offenbach kissed the lady to convey his supposed regret, which was a bad idea.

Beth Ingersoll was a much-neglected wife, and knew her way around male anatomy. Her touch was bold and intimate, and Offenbach was easily inspired.

"You can spend another quarter hour with the philosophers, Absalom. I believe your exertions in the saddle room didn't last even half that long."

Her bedroom had that musty, after-sex scent, the sheets no longer felt fresh, and too many days of too much drink had left Offenbach with a pounding headache. Then too, tomorrow weighed on him heavily.

He had a countess to ruin, else he would not be engaged in the current heroics.

"Intensity adds spice to an encounter," he said. "I really must be going. You will do your bit tomorrow?"

"Do your bit now, and we'll talk about tomorrow." She swung a leg over him, and Offenbach wondered if this was how a trained hunt horse felt later in the season.

Not this again. Not with you, of the rough hands and incessant demands.

"My love," Offenbach said. "I truly cannot tarry. I promise you, tomorrow night I will be entirely yours, provided all goes well during the scavenger hunt."

"Very well," she said, sitting back squarely on his sore and weary member. "But be prepared to acquit yourself well when next you're in this bed. I'd like to remember you *most* fondly."

While he'd like to forget he'd ever met her. "And I you, my dear." He patted her bum, nearly desperate to get her off of him.

She rose slowly, as if she knew his true feelings, which she could not possibly. He felt sorry for her, to be honest, and he was utterly disgusted with himself. For Mr. Terrence Cargill he felt neither pity nor disgust, but rather, violent loathing.

Offenbach made himself dress slowly, made himself endure much petting and kissing and a few grating giggles, and then he was free, out into the cool shadows of the corridors. He really ought to drop by the library. He had an incriminating note to write, and needed to do it when nobody else was about.

He descended to the floor below, only to meet young Lord Cargill on the landing.

"Offenbach, ready to call it a night?"

Cargill didn't sniff, but Offenbach knew the reek of trysting was in the air. Perfume, sweat, despair…

And shame. "I suppose I am. I will be relieved when this gathering concludes, no insult intended to present company."

"No insult taken." Cargill started down the corridor and Offenbach wandered along with him. Bed—clean sheets all to himself, no giggling or passionate moaning—loomed like the greatest treasure on earth. He could write his note tomorrow morning, before anybody else was about.

Now, he needed his rest.

∽

If Montmarche allowed the firelight to work its kind magic, he could envision Daphne Cargill as a younger woman. Still petite, perhaps more vivacious, perhaps a bit slimmer. Her gaze would not have held such depths of humor and wisdom though, nor the guarded self-possession a woman learned later in life.

He wanted that older, wiser, equally precious woman. He wanted a lover who wasn't comparing him to all the strutting Adonises, who sought his company as much as she longed for the bodily pleasure he could give her.

"You want me," he said, "and I desire you as well." He rose, keeping her hand in his. "Shall I lock the door?"

Some things didn't change, no matter how mature or self-confident a man became. Asking a woman to become his lover still took courage, and still left Lysander torn between joyous anticipation and anxious hope. The power was all hers in that instant, and he wouldn't want it any other way.

She came up against him, laying her cheek against his heart. "Lock the door in a moment."

Exactly. He wanted a woman who knew enough to savor the steps of the dance. Daphne rested against him, giving them both time to gather their courage—Montmarche could not have named the last woman with whom he'd been intimate—and to revel in thoughts of what was to come.

She untied the sash of his dressing gown and tucked in close, and what a delight, that they both wore only nightclothes, which were easily and quickly shed.

"So warm," she said, slipping her arms around him. "So wonderfully warm."

"So soft," he replied, kissing her cheek. "So wonderfully soft." And curved and feminine.

They smiled at each other, and Lysander drew back to lock the sitting room door. Daphne waited for him, and then he led her into his bedroom.

She stopped at the foot of his bed. "We should bind ourselves together at the wrist with the sash of your dressing gown, else I shall lose you in the vast reaches of this... slumbering earl park."

"You shall not lose me," Lysander said, closing the bedroom door. "I'll remain in plain view at all times." Within snuggling distance, to be exact.

Daphne took up the warming pan and shoveled coals into it. "If you'd like to disappear behind the privacy screen for a moment, I'll tend to the sheets."

He tarried to turn down the quilts with her, so she could warm the whole bed. Lysander usually ran the warmer over his half, then got a rude shock when he stuck a foot across the middle of the mattress.

No rude shocks tonight. Only pleasure.

"There," she said, heaving the quilts back up to the pillows. "Be quick please. I have plans for you."

Her plans, Lysander suspected, were plans for one night. His were more ambitious. If she'd have him, he'd start a courtship in the next hour, and embark on a partnership that rested on more than a compunction to secure the earldom's succession. George was equal to that task, and the family would be financially secure regardless of the fate of the title.

If the past two weeks had shown Lysander one thing, it was that he was ready to risk his heart again, because the right woman had at last come along.

He tended to his ablutions, and paused a moment to regard the fellow in the mirror. Aging well, but aging, and what of it? Of all the men who'd ever panted at her heels, Daphne Cargill had chosen *him* to gift with her favors.

An echo of a younger man's insouciance smiled back at him. *Don't muck this up, and do enjoy the hell out of it.* When he returned to the bed, Daphne was already under the covers, her dressing gown draped across the foot of the bed, her nightgown atop it.

"Bed curtains open or closed?" Lysander asked.

"Open please. The night is mild."

She wasn't shy about the firelight. Lysander laid his dressing gown atop hers, and pulled his nightshirt off before climbing under the covers.

Because he wasn't shy about the firelight either—not with her. She cuddled up against his side, he wrapped an arm around her shoulders, and a sense of sweetness and gratitude welled.

So comfortable, so easy, and so lovely. "Anything I need to know?" he asked, kissing her temple. "Your ribs are ticklish, you like to be whispered to in naughty French, that sort of thing?"

"I hardly remember." A pause. "Perhaps I ought not to have said that, but it's the truth. I have been a pattern card of widowed rectitude, lest Terrence have me sent to Yorkshire in disgrace. I also, to heap honesty on top of plain speaking, simply haven't been tempted."

How she flattered him. Lysander rolled to his side and wrapped her close. "To hell with Terrence, and Yorkshire, and for right now, rectitude. Can we agree on that?"

Daphne kissed him, smack on the mouth, no wandering around his cheeks or brow working up to it. "We are agreed. My ribs are not ticklish." She ran her foot up his calf, or rather, her thick wool stocking. "My feet tend to be cold, in only the physical sense."

I am in love. I am in love with a woman who wears her stockings to bed with me, because that's who she is and she's happy with herself.

"Thank God it's only in the physical sense." He kissed her back, taking his time, letting the warmth and wonder spread through him. Daphne was enthusiastic without being impatient, which was perfect.

And her hands… she had a wonderful touch, as if she listened with her fingers and palms as she shaped his shoulders, his hips, the muscles and contours of his back. Warm hands, and generous with the pleasure they conjured.

"You," she said, patting his bum. "Now. Please."

He smiled against her mouth. "I was hoping you'd ask." He was aroused, and more than that, he was passionately eager to join with her. He wanted the great crescendo, the cascading pleasure, but he also wanted the quiet aftermath and the sweet touches.

With her, Lysander wanted the whole measure of joy. If he was lucky, she wanted that too, and not only for one night.

He shifted so he was over her, tucked close enough to nuzzle at the orange blossom scented join of her neck and shoulder. "I am tempted to make stirring declarations."

She laughed, her belly bouncing against his. "You can dispense with the words and make the declarations with your body instead."

Excellent suggestion. He sank into her slowly, his movements modest the better to make the joining pleasurable for her. A sigh fanning past his ear suggested he'd got this much right.

"Daphne?"

"Mmmm."

"If you're inclined to move with me, I'd like that."

A sleeping queen awoke in his arms, fitting her rhythm to his so exquisitely he had to focus mentally on counting her breaths lest he hasten to completion. How wonderful—how marvelously, delightfully exquisite, to have that challenge again.

"Name," she whispered, locking her ankles at the small of his back.

Name? *Name?* "Lysander."

"Fits you." She wrapped her hand around his nape and kissed

him just as he felt satisfaction overtake her. That kiss was nearly his undoing, a kiss for the ages, a kiss to remind a man of all the wonders of creation, but he switched to counting in Latin, and preserved control.

Barely.

"Lysander," she said, his name never before having been such a benediction. "I had forgotten much. You remind me so sweetly."

"Allow me to remind you again."

No daring feats of loverly restraint this time. He approached this interlude with purpose, and she gave as good as she got, until she wrapped him in a ferocious embrace and shuddered against him once more. He withdrew and spent on her belly, the repletion magnificent in its intensity.

"Now you are reminded as well," she said, her fingers drifting through his hair. "I need to hold you."

He crouched over her, breathing like a winded steeplechaser. "I need to hold you as well." *All night long.*

"Handkerchief, please, my lord."

Right. But where...?

She kissed his wrist, for he was braced with a forearm on either side of her hand. "On the bedside table."

He spied the desired linen. "I suppose you expect me to reach for it, and me in such a weakened condition?"

She hugged him with her legs, a good strong squeeze. "If you wouldn't mind. I'm too satisfied to reach for anything but you."

He sat back and passed her the handkerchief, frankly admiring her breasts while she tidied up, and then—oh, then—she made a few passes with the cloth at his fading arousal, and angels sang naughty thoughts in his imagination.

"Thank you," he said, taking the cloth from her and tossing it onto the bedside table. "Thank you, exceedingly. Cuddle up."

"You cuddle up too," she said, resuming her place against his side.

"Gladly." He was tempted to make those stirring declarations now, to lay his heart at her feet and embark on the delightful business of planning their future.

"I will never begrudge Mrs. Ingersoll her raptures again," Daphne said. "I feel as if I'd like to run yodeling through the corridors that house parties are wonderful, and you are wonderful, and all of creation is wonderful. My offspring would be mortified."

"I would be flattered, and I daresay you'd surprise more than a few of the guests."

"Don't worry," she said, patting his chest. "I am the soul of discretion. Also blissfully relaxed."

Sleep tugged at Lysander, but so did a sense that he was allowing an opportunity to slip past him. He cast about for a way to broach the topic of a courtship, for he would not be cheated out of a period of doting swain-hood.

One embarked on that course by asking to pay a lady addresses. Such a question was generally asked while both parties were clothed, probably to spare a man much embarrassment if he'd misread the situation.

Had he mis-read the situation? "Daphne?"

She breathed in a slow easy rhythm, an inert length of well-pleasured female warm against his side.

"My dear?"

Nothing, not even a murmur.

"Ah, well. In the morning then." He kissed her cheek and let dreams of doting swain-hood claim him.

∽

Daphne had been greedy, making love with Montmarche again in the middle of the night, the sort of dreamy, half-aware pleasuring that brought smiles when recalled the next day. She'd also accepted his overtures as the first hint of gray pearled the eastern horizon, though she should not have.

The knowledge of impending parting gilded her satisfaction with sorrow and frustration, even as she drowsed in Montmarche's bed. He had allowed himself the proverbial stolen moment with a willing widow. Maybe that was his version of a fling before yielding once again to the bonds of matrimony.

Or maybe not. He was a sumptuous lover, attentive and considerate with enough imagination to keep a lady very, very interested. He'd also been more than that though... He'd been affectionate, tender, *doting*.

"I should be going," Daphne said, making no move to leave the bed.

"Must you?"

A gentleman's answer. "My good name means much to me, your lordship, and the scavenger hunt is today. Your guests will be up and about early." Though not this early. The house party schedule meant breakfast had not yet been laid out.

"The voice of reason is an unwelcome addition to any tryst." He was spooned around her, a comfy blanket of lover, and gave her a long hug. "I have enjoyed this night more than I can possibly say."

He let go of her, while Daphne fumbled for a reply. "Likewise, your lordship. Unlooked for delight that will be much savored in memory."

"You are lordshipping me and we haven't even put our clothes on. Do you know how primness when you're naked inspires my manly humors?"

"We haven't time for a demonstration, sir." More's the pity.

He let her go. "Very well, then away with you." He took her hand and kissed her knuckles, his smile wicked and sleepy.

"Wretch." Daphne tossed back the covers and began the trek to the far side of the bed. She grabbed her nightgown on the way, and pulled it over her head. The step was on the earl's side, so she slid down from the mattress, her heels hitting the carpet with a soft thump.

Montmarche left the bed more decorously, then paused to scratch his chest and stretch before shrugging into his dressing gown.

Daphne indulged a gawk and liked what she saw very much. She would miss him, and this memory, as precious as it was, would be bittersweet.

"I could ring for a tray," he said, holding up Daphne's dressing gown. "The maid leaves it in the sitting room, and nobody will suspect that I've had company in my bed." He smoothed Daphne's dressing gown over her shoulders, the gesture so casually affectionate she nearly asked him to do it again.

"The sooner I am back in my own quarters, the better." She went up on her toes to kiss him, a peck on the cheek lest her resolve weaken.

"Very well, madam." He grasped the ends of her sash and belted the dressing gown. "But I'm walking you to your door. If anybody asks, we met down in the breakfast parlor where we stole an early cup of tea rather than bother the staff on such a busy day."

Daphne's mind went where it always did: *What would Terrence think of me larking about in my dressing gown, except a dressing gown was decent, if highly informal, attire.*

To blazes with Terrence for once. "I will appreciate your escort." Though being seen in dishabille with the earl was a risk—a small risk.

He wrapped her in an embrace, which Daphne took for a bodily request to remain present with him for at least the space of one more shared hug.

"We will talk further of what has transpired here, my lady. I am mindful that neither of us shared our favors lightly."

He could not possibly want her for a mistress, nor would she be his mistress, so what on earth was that declaration about?

"Prior to this encounter, I hadn't shared my favors *at all*," Daphne said. "But I have no regrets about being your lover. None."

The light in his eyes changed, from pleased to thoughtful, with a possible hint of frustration. Maybe that wasn't what he'd wanted to hear, but they had no time left for flirtatious discussion.

"Thank you." He stepped back just as Daphne would have clung for yet more stolen moments, then they were walking side by side through the shadowed corridor.

Half the sconces had guttered, which was a kindness preserving the sense of nocturnal privacy. The distance from his room to hers was too short, though all was silence as Daphne paused with Montmarche outside her door.

"Thank you," she said, giving Montmarche's words back to him. She gave him the embrace as well, wrapping her arms around him, and holding on for a last, lovely hug. She would treasure this night for the rest of her life, and regret that she wasn't to treasure the man as well.

Montmarche held her close, as if he'd imprint her form on his memory. "We have more to say to each other, but now is not the time. You will haunt me until next we meet."

Over his shoulder Daphne caught a movement in the gloom. White linen, pale breeches.

Offenbach, damn him for all eternity. As quickly as she'd spotted him, he drew back. The earl would not have seen him, but Daphne surely had.

She ended the embrace and opened her door. "Farewell, my lord."

Montmarche bowed, the dressing gown giving his courtesy a regal air. "Farewell, for now."

Daphne closed her door, locked it, and listened for the earl's footsteps to fade. Offenbach's word alone would not condemn her—his reputation preceded him to that extent—but if Offenbach could inspire others to find fault with Daphne's behavior, she'd have a fight on her hands.

"So be it," she informed her cold, empty sitting room. "What's one more skirmish?"

Though why, why on God's green and beautiful earth, should she have to fight at all?

"The scavenger hunt is today," Sophronia said. "Papa has said I may watch from the schoolroom." She'd watched last evening as the gardeners and footmen had secreted various objects about the grounds, though the rules of the game according to Aunt Cassandra meant teams could only search the public rooms, terraces, and formal gardens for the items on their lists.

Henderson gave Sophronia's porridge a stir. "You would have watched from underfoot otherwise. When your papa took his leave of you yesterday, he told me that if you maintain good behavior this morning, you are to join the company this afternoon for the picnic."

The day was already beautiful, as only Marche Hall on a fine day could be beautiful. The nursery windows were open, the trill of birdsong and the scent of scythed meadows wafting in a soft breeze.

"Papa said I could *attend the picnic*?"

Henderson's smile was rare and kind. "You have tried very hard these past two weeks, my lady. It's not my place to say, but I think you should be proud of yourself."

The scent of cinnamon rose from the bowl before Sophronia, and normally, she loved her morning porridge, but this news was too exciting.

"Do you think Papa is proud of me? Is that why he's taken to visiting the nursery?" He came by at no set time, though for the duration of the house party, he'd been making regular appearances in the East Wing. Sophronia feared the visits would stop when the guests departed, but she did not know how to ask her Papa to continue looking in on her.

Henderson poured herself a cup of tea and added milk and sugar. She was a stout, calm young woman, and without the Dreaded Dagmire smacking everything with her birch rod, Henderson had become friendlier too.

"The earl is a busy man. He would not come by on a whim, child. Eat your porridge."

Sophronia wanted to gulp down her breakfast so she could dance around the schoolroom, but that would be silly. Papa might come by and catch her capering around like a spring lamb.

"Lady Cargill said I have promise as an artist," Sophronia said. "I showed Papa my drawings, and he said I have a keen eye for equestrian anatomy. What does that mean?"

"You should ask him, though I think it means you draw horses well."

"Sindri is handsome."

Henderson scowled at her tea. "Handsome is as handsome does. I will be glad when this house party is concluded. Poor staff is run off their feet, and such goings on..."

"You mean like Mr. Offenbach kissing everybody?" Sophronia had kept an eye on him such as she was able to.

Henderson set her cup on its saucer. "You are growing up too fast, my lady. Mr. Offenbach is a bachelor. They sometimes forget themselves."

Mr. Offenbach had forgotten himself with Mrs. Ingersoll, Miss Tremont, and Mrs. Hofstra, that Sophronia knew of. The nursery windows overlooked the gardens, maze, and tree line, and much of the house party had unfolded beneath Sophronia's envious eye.

Lord Cargill liked to take a sketch pad into the garden. He rode occasionally too, though his horse was not so fine as Papa's.

Cousin Helena and Mr. Prescott had forgotten themselves near the laburnum alley twice, and Mrs. Cavanaugh seemed compelled to sit along various garden paths with a book, but she seldom turned a page.

Lady Cargill had taken her easel into the park on several occasions, and Sophronia had resisted—mightily—the temptation to sneak out through the scent garden and join her.

"I forget myself too," Sophronia said. "I don't go around kissing people when I do."

"No," Henderson replied. "You merely get grass stains on your pinny, neglect to put your table napkin on your lap, and switch to French without realizing it."

Sophronia checked and found her napkin exactly where it should be. "Papa understands my French." He answered Sophronia in French as well, which made her feel very grown up.

"Your porridge will get cold," Henderson said. "The guests will take a late breakfast today and then embark on the scavenger hunt. The picnic won't start until two of the clock so we'd best plan to keep you occupied until then, lest you disappoint your papa."

Sophronia's porridge was already cooling, though it still tasted good. "I will write a letter to Lady Cargill, to send after the house party. She said I could, and she will write back. I can also practice the pianoforte—did you know that Papa can play the pianoforte?—and then I will sketch the gardens during the scavenger hunt and wave to anybody who sees me."

"A fine plan," Henderson said, topping up her tea cup. "I foresee a wonderful afternoon for you, my lady, and for all of his lordship's guests, too."

CHAPTER EIGHT

Daphne had avoided joining the company for breakfast, though she could not avoid the scavenger hunt. This was the last informal entertainment of the gathering, the day was fine, and nobody would believe she had a megrim or turned ankle.

She took a tray in her room—even merry widows caught out in their frolics must eat—and alternately fretted and fumed.

Why had Offenbach been lurking in the corridor before anybody else was awake? Had he been able to identify the earl as Daphne's escort? What gossip would ensue, or could Offenbach's silence be bought with a reciprocal offer of discretion? Mrs. Ingersoll was married, after all.

Such thoughts were distasteful, and fueled the ire that simmered along with Daphne's worry. Why, when she'd for once allowed herself some pleasure, must Offenbach slither into her garden, turning what should have been a lovely interlude into something tawdry and regrettable?

"Except I don't regret a moment of it," she informed her reflection in the cheval mirror. She was the same Lady Cargill she'd been yesterday, and yet, she was a different Daphne. She'd known pleasure and intimacy and the ease of being lovers with Montmarche.

"Offenbach shall not tarnish that gift, no matter what tattle he threatens to whisper into Terrence's ear."

She grabbed a parasol, stuffed a pair of crocheted gloves in her skirt pocket, and headed for the door.

"Mama." Phoebe stood in the corridor, Charles at her elbow. "We were concerned when you didn't come down to breakfast."

Charles bowed. "You are in good looks today, Mother."

Charles was in good looks too. A fortnight of fresh air and socializing had brightened his smile, and even Phoebe looked happy.

If Offenbach thinks he can imperil my children's happiness, I will make him regret the very notion.

"It's a beautiful day," Daphne said. "And we have treasure to hunt. Has Lady Cassandra passed out the lists?"

"Lord Montmarche will hand them around on the back terrace shortly," Phoebe said, linking arms with Daphne and starting for the stairs. "He and her ladyship are to referee, because it wouldn't be fair for them to participate. They know the house and grounds too well."

Daphne had also hidden in her room because she had not wanted to face Montmarche with others about. For as long as possible, she wanted to put off acknowledging that the role of lover was a brief aberration for them both. This morning they were host and guest, earl and viscountess, and those roles must be resumed.

Though he had promised her further discussion, likely an awkward acknowledgement of theoretical consequences. Conception was unlikely, given the precautions Montmarche had taken, and Daphne's increasingly unreliable menses.

And no, that evidence of aging biology did not make her sad. It made her relieved.

"I have enjoyed myself more at this gathering than I'd thought possible," Phoebe said. "The weather has cooperated of course, but the company has also been congenial."

Charles propped a hip on the bannister and slid down to the

landing. "I've had a pleasant time as well, but could have wished for a different roommate. Offenbach came and went at all hours and was forever attempting to lead me astray."

"You don't lead astray very well," Daphne said, resisting the urge to fuss at his hair. "Typical Cargill."

Though she had allowed herself to become intimate with Montmarche, and she did not regret that departure from strict propriety *at all*.

"I do hope I'm on Mr. Tremont's team," Phoebe said. "He's sensible. He'll have a plan for how we find all the items."

"He's not bad-looking either," Charles said, smiling a little-brother-knows-all smile. "And a fine fellow too."

"You, on the other hand," Phoebe said, pausing on the last stair, "are entirely awful. I hope your team loses badly."

They smiled at each other, when a year ago, they might have stuck out their tongues.

"My team will win," Daphne said, "because it's *my* team."

They emerged onto the back terrace, where most of the guests were already assembled. Many of the men were in riding attire after a morning hack, while the ladies had donned walking dresses. The mood was cheerful and chattery.

Montmarche stood near the balustrade. He too was in riding attire, his hair a trifle windblown, his hands bare. Mrs. Ingersoll flanked him on one side, Mrs. Cavanaugh on the other. He had not spotted Daphne, and that was fortunate, for she needed a moment to gather her fortitude.

Montmarche was attractive, he was good company, and he was everything Daphne could wish for in a lover. How did he feel about her? As Mrs. Ingersoll went into peals of grating laughter, Daphne resolved to at least have that discussion with Montmarche.

She could not risk scandal, but for Lysander, she could risk her dignity.

"That laughter will haunt me," Phoebe muttered. "I don't think she can help herself."

"Then she oughtn't to laugh at all," Charles replied. "Not gentlemanly of me, I know."

"Let's find our teams," Daphne said. "And prepare for guile and experience to once more triumph over youth and ignorance."

The children moved away, while Daphne looked for a place to be inconspicuous. Why had she not sketched Montmarche while she'd had the chance? She took a seat at an empty table beneath a balcony, the better to study her subject.

He'd moved on to a knot of men, Mr. Tremont and Mr. Prescott among them. The younger fellows showed Montmarche deference, in their posture, in their willingness to yield him the floor.

"Good morning, my lady."

Daphne had been so absorbed memorizing the contour of Montmarche's shoulders that Mr. Offenbach's greeting startled her.

"Sir. Good morning." *Go away and stay away.*

"You need not worry that I'll be indiscreet," he said. "Far from it. What's life without an occasional diversion?"

"Mr. Offenbach, I don't know what you saw, or what you thought you saw, but this topic does not interest me." She could *not* cause a scene, and Offenbach likely knew that.

"I thought Mrs. Cavanaugh had got her hooks into Montmarche," Offenbach went on as if Daphne hadn't spoken. "Lord knows the lady hasn't the time of day for the likes of me. I'm dirt beneath her shoe. But all along you were having your wicked way with the very proper earl. Enterprising of you, I say."

"The less you say, the better. Mrs. Ingersoll has had an exceedingly agreeable time at this gathering, largely thanks to you."

Offenbach's smile was unnervingly friendly. "I have nothing to gain by attempting to ruin you, my lady. Not one thing. If I were to make accusations, my word would be worthless compared to the standing of mine host. Montmarche would skewer me with a rusty pike before all of polite society. You're safe, while I must contend with creditors of a most unsympathetic nature."

Daphne did not trust Offenbach any farther than she could toss her parasol, but he seemed to be in earnest.

"Do you harbor a *tendresse* for Mrs. Cavanaugh?" she asked. "You have a very odd way of showing it, Mr. Offenbach."

"She can't ignore me when I'm being outrageous," he said, rising. "But no. I know better than to pine for what I do not deserve. I'll wish you good morning, my lady, and good hunting."

The phrase jarred, though Daphne had used it herself. She declined to offer Offenbach her hand, and was still sitting alone under the balcony five minutes later when Rehobeth Ingersoll settled into the seat beside her.

"Montmarche isn't on a team," Mrs. Ingersoll said. "Why do you suppose that is?"

"Because as owner of the property, he'd have an advantage in any game that depended on searching the premises."

"Or he's made other plans for the morning. I'm to give you this." She passed Daphne a folded piece of paper. "And you must not worry, my lady. I enjoy my little peccadilloes, but I can keep my mouth shut."

The note was sealed with the Montmarche crest, and Lysander had been standing with Mrs. Ingersoll not ten minutes ago.

"I suspect you'll want to read that somewhere very private," Mrs. Ingersoll said. "House parties can be so amusing, can't they?"

She patted Daphne's arm and wafted away, yoo-hooing to Mr. Tremont and Mr. Gavineau.

Daphne opened the note, holding it out of sight below the table.

My dove,

Meet me in the maze and we'll lose ourselves in passion. Until we can scale the heights of pleasure, I remain...

Ever thine

. . .

My dove? Lysander had not once, in an entire night of lovemaking, used an endearment with Daphne. Not my dove, not precious, not darling, not anything more personal than *my dear*. Moreover, the maze was forbidden to guests, and if two rational adults sought to lose themselves in passion, Marche Hall boasted an embarrassment of bedrooms, linen closets, sitting rooms, and deserted stairways that offered better accommodations.

"Mama," Phoebe called from across the terrace. "The teams are forming. Come draw a number."

Daphne waved and smiled, but she did not leave her seat. Montmarche would never have sealed a note with his crest if he sought to be discreet. Two people Daphne did not trust had told her not to worry, and then she'd been given a note that made no sense.

She was worried.

∽

Daphne hadn't come down to breakfast, and now she lurked beneath a balcony, refusing to greet her host. A younger man, a man with less experience of the world, might have worried.

Lysander was admittedly *concerned*. Any conscientious host should take note of a guest reluctant to join the day's diversion, but the truth was, this guest had become his lover, and he hoped very much she wasn't regretting her generosity.

First Offenbach and then Mrs. Ingersoll had briefly joined Daphne, and when Cassandra would have entangled Lysander in a discussion of silk versus lace parasols, he excused himself.

"I must see to my other guests." He bowed generally, and made his escape. As he threaded his way across the terrace, Daphne remained beneath the balcony, perhaps waiting for him.

Or avoiding him. "My lady." He bowed over her hand. "You are in radiant good looks this morning."

She smiled. "I probably look a bit short of sleep, but then, so do you, and we are both happier for it. Can you spare me a moment, my lord?"

He could spare her the rest of his life. The longer he'd considered that plan, the more joyously he contemplated it. He took the place beside her, and to blazes with anybody who noticed that he was enjoying a conversation tête-à-tête with her ladyship.

"Are you happier for having enjoyed my company last night, my lady?"

She laid her parasol on the table—neither silk nor lace, but rather, sensible cotton. "I am. I had forgotten how sumptuous the pleasure is with the right person. How deeply gratifying the affection."

Sumptuous was encouraging. "Passion is wasted on the young. I too was reminded of simple and profound joys."

He gathered up his courage, and reached for her hand just as she brandished a scrap of paper.

"This note," she said, at the same time he ventured forth with, "Do you ever wonder if—?"

They both fell silent and she passed him the note.

He scanned the few words, though he did not recognize the hand. "Good gracious. Somebody is violating my clear and oft-repeated admonition not to explore the maze."

"The note was sealed with your crest, my lord, and put into my hands. If the note is from you, then I can assure you, I am not a silly girl who must be enticed into folly with stolen glimpses of your forbidden maze."

Lysander read over the note again. He'd never, not in his most callow youth, written such drivel. "You've seen a bit more than my maze already, madam, and anybody could find a Montmarche seal in the library or the morning room. Is there some other fellow who might be sending you such notes?" For her sake he hoped not. Also for his own sake.

Maudlin tripe.

"Nobody should send me such notes. I suspect Offenbach of

attempting to lure me into an indiscretion so he can publicly humiliate me."

"Lure you, by making use of my seal?"

She nodded, looking regal and peevish as she surveyed the terrace. "He saw us, when you so gallantly escorted me back to my room. I wasn't sure he recognized you—your back was to him—but he apparently did."

Well, well, well. "You avoided breakfast because you did not want to confront Offenbach?"

Her gaze traveled over Lysander. "He's the type to pass along snide innuendo with the toast and marmalade. I suspect he pines from afar for what he cannot have."

He cannot have you. Lysander was surprised—and pleased—with the vehemence of that sentiment. "Offenbach needs a good hiding, and I am tempted to give it to him. Luring you into the maze is a desperate and despicable act."

Daphne's smile was faint, but it was a smile. "You are so fierce."

"From you, on this beautiful morning, I would rather hear myself described as passionate, but fierce will suffice. While you…"

"Yes?" She cocked her head, clearly willing to hear a bit of flummery so early in the day.

Lysander took her hand and kissed her knuckles. "You are an absolute diamond, and I have a blasted scavenger hunt to manage when I would rather… Suffice to say, that if I didn't think your son would interrogate me the livelong day as to my prospects and provenance, I would ask the lad for permission to court you."

Daphne sat up quite straight. "Court me?"

"My skills are rusty, but once upon a time, I could manage a whole quadrille without once crashing into my partner. I am a competent accompanist, and I can read poetry in French or English, though I don't always grasp the French double entendres."

"What has French poetry to do with…?" She waved a hand in the general direction of the bedrooms on the next floor up.

"Precisely. I might not be all that impressive as a suitor, but I aspire to make you a devoted, fierce, *and* passionate husband. Will you give me leave to hope?"

In the time it took her to fold up the little note and pull on her gloves, Lysander realized that even if he could have turned back the clock, to be a more dashing suitor or tireless lover, he would rather have the wisdom and resilience that came with age.

Daphne might turn him down, and perhaps they'd become one of those older demi-couples who were invited everywhere together, without anybody having to make a great to-do over it.

She might make him work for it, withholding a decision for a time; and work for it, he would.

Or she might, possibly, if he was very lucky, say...

"Yes." Her smile was luminous and full of mischief. "You have reason to hope and aspire and even swagger a bit, discreetly, of course. One doesn't want the young fellows to be cast in the shade by your gallantry."

Gallant fellow that he was, Lysander collected the note, lest it fall into the wrong hands. "You are not succumbing to temptation in a weak moment? I have a ten-year-old hoyden in my nursery, and I'm not much of one for the Town whirl."

Daphne leaned close. "I *despise* the Town whirl. I do my duty because Phoebe needs a chaperone, but I'm hopeful she and Mr. Tremont might make a match of it. What do we do with that note, my lord? I would not mind leaving Mr. Offenbach to wander your maze for all eternity, except that your gardeners would eventually stumble on his bones."

"To blazes with Offenbach and his bones. You'll marry me, then?"

She gathered up her parasol. "If I were twenty-five years younger, I'd hesitate and stammer and allude to the need to get to know you better, but those twenty-five years are lost to me. I know my own heart and mind. We will suit, my lord, and I adore the hoyden in your nursery."

"Then I have already found the only treasure on this property worth having."

They beamed at each other for a moment, not fatuously of course, because fatuousness was the province of callow swains and blushing damsels. Perhaps their beaming was a bit fierce.

Lysander rose and offered the lady his hand. "What do you suppose Offenbach pines for?"

"Not a what, a who. He's ridden the hobbyhorse of the charming wastrel until the beast is ready to collapse from over-exertion, and now... He's in the grip of bad habits and poor prospects. Mr. Offenbach wants a wife. A sensible woman like Mrs. Cavanaugh, who has a way with unruly boys and unrulier men. He knows she'd be a good companion, and I believe, given the chance, he'd try hard to be a decent spouse to her."

"I grant you, Offenbach is charming and handsome enough, but Emma Cavanaugh would not allow Absalom Offenbach within kissing distance if he were the last eligible..." Lysander fell silent, because clearly, Mrs. Cavanaugh viewed husbands as projects, and Offenbach was in desperate need of a project manager.

"I have an idea," he said, tucking Daphne's hand over his arm. "Do you suppose my George would deliver a note if you asked him to?"

"A note to Mrs. Cavanaugh? He could certainly manage the requisite discretion."

"Exactly so. I'm not suggesting we matchmake, precisely, but two people stuck in the same maze should at least strike up a conversation, don't you think? A conversation is a good place to start."

Daphne paused to open her parasol. "A conversation would be a novel experience for Offenbach when it comes to private situations and females. Who knows? Away from prying eyes and gossips, he and Mrs. Cavanaugh might find something to discuss."

"Or she might black his eye."

Daphne positioned her parasol over her shoulder and took

Lysander's arm. "She has four sons. I suspect she'll deliver a swift kick to his expectations if he oversteps."

Marriage to this woman would be enchanting. "I will tear the seal away, and Ever Thine Offenbach can try his luck scaling the heights of conversation with Mrs. Cavanaugh."

Lysander and his intended—his intended!—strolled across the terrace and down into the gardens, and perhaps it was simply the relief of a house party drawing to close, or perhaps it was the salubrious effect of the fresh morning air, but his gardens hadn't look half so pretty to him at any point in the past five years.

∽

Daphne hadn't felt half so pretty for years. She'd grown accustomed to blending in, to being graciously forgettable, but oh, how the prospect of marriage to Lysander pleased her. The physical intimacy was lovely to contemplate, but so too was the prospect of a marital friendship.

A compatriot in life, a hand to hold, a partner in parenting and domesticity, much less in sickness and in health.

And the idea that Terrence would finally have to manage on his own means was so great a relief that Daphne could acknowledge how badly he'd been bedeviling her.

"May we tell the children tonight?" Daphne asked. "Before dinner. I don't want to make any announcements, because this is a wedding party, and the bride and groom should have all the good wishes, but I want..."

"You want the children to stop worrying about us. I daresay my sister will claim she chose us for each other. There's George. Killoway, rather."

Daphne dealt with the note, which George agreed to pass along to Mrs. Cavanaugh on behalf of "another guest."

"Shall we do the banns," Daphne asked, returning to Lysander's side, "or use a special license?"

Lysander set a leisurely pace along the garden path, and Daphne suspected he was showing her off to the groups milling about, waiting for the scavenger hunt to begin. Truth be told, she was showing him off too.

"You will be my bride, if God allows and you remain willing. The particulars of the ceremony must fall within your demesne. I would honestly enjoy..." He scowled faintly, as if searching for words.

"Yes?"

He twirled his wrist. "A few stolen kisses, some sweet nothings, a billet-doux, though you are most likely to end up with a description of the harvest or fall lambing from me. I shall make the effort, nonetheless, but don't expect any of that ever-thine folderol."

He wanted... he wanted some *romance*. "Of course not. We need time for the children to adjust to the notion of our marriage, and for us to work out the practical considerations."

"Precisely. We have lives, and weaving them together will take some thought." He bent to pluck a pink rose from the trellis arched over the walkway and passed the bloom to Daphne.

She chose another blossom and tucked it into his lapel. "Banns then," she said. "We are in no hurry, are we?"

"None at all, provided you don't expect me to wait until the wedding night to further demonstrate my impressive ferocity."

He was so very dear. "Do you *want* to wait until the wedding night, my lord?"

"Build up the anticipation, you mean?"

"Something like that."

He drew her to a halt and regarded her with a brooding frown. "Frankly, no. I am already in such a state of anticipation that I doubt my ability to withstand weeks in the same condition. If the maze were not spoken for, I'd invite you to slip away with me there, and we would *all the pleasures prove*."

"You quote me poetry."

"The alternative is profanity. If this scavenger hunt doesn't soon get under way, I will have a stern word with my darling sister."

"She might be waiting for me to return you to the terrace, Montmarche."

He glanced up at the terrace, where Mrs. Gavineau stood calling out names to the knot of guests around her.

Lysander kissed Daphne on the cheek and he took his time about it too. "*Now*, you may return me to the assemblage who have been ogling our every move, but do not think to abandon me to search for feathers and speckled pebbles."

She would like to hunt for treasure in his bed, which was very naughty of her. "I have been assigned to a team, my lord."

"So was Mrs. Cavanaugh, and so was Offenbach, but I don't see them among the scavengers, do you?"

Daphne looked about the terrace, seeing neither Mrs. Cavanaugh nor Mr. Offenbach waiting with the crowd preparing to start the scavenger hunt. "If they are in the maze, you will rescue them once the guests have dispersed?"

"I suppose I ought to."

"You really should, sir. Before luncheon at the latest."

"Or before supper, if the weather holds fair."

"Naughty man."

"For you, my dear, I am prepared to be very naughty indeed."

Silly banter. Daphne had missed it more than she'd known.

The teams were large enough that nobody was inclined to remark the half dozen or so guests not present, and after the rules had been read at length, and good wishes and the requisite taunts exchanged, the teams prepared to move off in search of the listed treasures.

Daphne remained happily at Lysander's side, even when Mrs. Gavineau aimed a rather puzzled smile at her.

"Papa! Papa!" Lady Sophronia pelted out the house. "You must come. Mr. Offenbach and Mrs. Cavanaugh are trapped in the maze and absolutely terrified." Every guest stared at the child, who was panting even as she tugged at her father's sleeve. "Please, Papa, you cannot leave them there."

Mrs. Gavineau touched Sophronia's shoulder. "How do you know they are terrified, child?"

"Because they are hugging each other mortally tight, and they haven't taken a step the whole time I tried to wave at them from the nursery windows. Mrs. Cavanaugh's hat fell off and she couldn't even let go of Mr. Offenbach to pick it up. *They are petrified* and we must rescue them."

A hum of conversation started up among the guests, while Mrs. Gavineau's expression went from curious, to aghast, to carefully blank.

"My friends, good luck on your scavenger hunt," Montmarche called. "Lady Sophronia and I have guests to rescue. Lady Cargill, if you'd accompany us?"

Sophronia capered ahead of them, while Daphne toddled along beside the earl. They made it halfway past the conservatory before they both went off into whoops.

EPILOGUE

By the time the ceremony concluded, Phoebe was weeping softly on Mr. Tremont's arm, George was looking serious, and Charles and Sophronia were apparently hatching up some plot involving decorations on the Montmarche traveling coach.

The chapel had become a busy place in recent weeks. Helena and Mr. Prescott's nuptials had begun the festivities. Mrs. Cavanaugh had made Mr. Offenbach the happiest of men thereafter, and now Daphne and Lysander had spoken their vows as well.

Phoebe and Mr. Tremont had chosen an autumn date, though Daphne suspected they'd anticipate their vows—or she rather hoped they would. Life was short and love should be enjoyed.

"Don't I get to kiss my bride?" Lysander asked, as the organist's recessional thundered through the little chapel. "I am certain there's a tradition, or there should be, about kissing the bride." He offered his arm, and smile to go with it that assured Daphne more than kissing would be involved in the nuptial celebrations.

"It's the bride who does the kissing," she said, leaning close. She paused for a moment on the altar steps, savoring the joy. The children were on their best behavior and turned out in their Sunday best.

Mr. and Mrs. Gavineau were indeed looking as proud as if they'd brought the happy couple together—this happy couple too—and Montmarche retainers of longstanding took up the remaining pews.

Lysander led her down the aisle and out in the bright sunshine. The party would walk back to the house for the wedding breakfast, followed by an open house for neighbors and friends.

"Why didn't we do as sensible couples do, and leave for the honey month directly after the wedding breakfast?" Daphne asked.

"Because we did not want to be exhausted by travel on our wedding night," Lysander said, pausing at the top of the church steps. "We did choose a beautiful wedding day, didn't we?"

He was doubtless thinking of his first wedding day, as Daphne had thought of hers. How could she not? That day had been full of joy and sunshine too, though viewed from the church steps, the memory was wistful.

One could not really embark on a second marriage without truly, absolutely ending the first. That was a sad thought, and one she knew Lysander would understand. She found him more than once in recent weeks sitting in solitude by the family plot.

"James would have liked you, Montmarche. He would have pronounced you a capital fellow."

"Maria would have approved of you too. Sophronia has already asked if she can call you mama."

"She told you that?"

"While we were riding yesterday. You were very wise to suggest I take her out regularly on horseback. She's a different girl when she starts the day with some fresh air."

Charles too, seemed to benefit from having a step-papa. The two fellows played cards in the library after supper most evenings, with Lord Killoway sometimes joining them. Daphne left the menfolk to their conversation and philosophizing, more grateful than she could say that Charles had the benefit of Lysander's wisdom before going up to university.

Daphne would have started up the path toward the house, but Lysander drew her to a halt. "About that kiss, Lady Montmarche."

"Lady Montmarche. I suppose that would be me." *Now,* that was her, though for years, the title had belonged to another. "I suppose I had best be about it."

She hesitated, and for no good reason at all, tears welled. On this beautiful day, on this happy occasion, she was about to bawl like Sophronia in a taking.

Lysander's gaze was patient and tender. "I know," he said, "I know the feelings are complicated, but today is a day to rejoice. My lady, look."

A pair of blue butterflies, anything but common, danced around Daphne's shoulders. One lit for a moment on her sleeve, then fluttered around Lysander, before winging away with its mate.

"If we were sentimental people," Daphne said, "we might consider that an encouraging sign."

"I wasn't sentimental. For too long, I denied myself that pleasure, but I am ready to make up for lost time now. Might you kiss me, my lady?"

She kissed him, and he kissed her, and the wedding guests clapped and whooped and made unseemly suggestions, and when the wedding night finally arrived, neither Lysander nor Daphne was exhausted, but they were both very, very sentimental.

And also *quite* fierce.

TO MY DEAR READERS

I hope you enjoyed this summer bagatelle, because I certainly had a good time writing it! Mary Balogh was actually my inspiration for writing a later-in-life couple (hers are wonderful), and I did very much enjoy Lysander and Daphne's wisdom, humor, and courage.

If you're looking for a longer read to tuck into your beach bag, I just released Lord Julian's ninth mystery, ***A Gentleman of Questionable Judgment***, which sees his lordship off to the races, where everybody is breaking the rules and nobody has a credible alibi. What's a sleuth to do? (Confide in his horse, of course).

August will see the release of Julian's tenth mystery, a ***Gentleman in Possession of Secrets (***missing spinster *and* a missing hoard of ancient gold). Then in September, it's back to our *Bad Heir Day Tales* with ***The Besotted Baron***, book four in that series.

So many fun stories, and plenty more to follow!

Happy reading!
    Grace Burrowes

Printed in Dunstable, United Kingdom